Mandel opened his briefcase and spread out a dozen documents on the President's desk. They were all marked:

TOP SECRET
Limited NATO Distribution

"This is the latest batch, Mr. President," Mandel said.

"Do you recognize these, General?" the President asked.

"Yes sir, Mr. President, I do, God help me."

The President turned back to Mandel. "They're Category Q documents, aren't they?"

"Yes sir," Mandel said.

"Where were they found?"

"On the body of a KGB courier in Paris."

"Exactly what are you saying, Mandel?" asked the President.

"In my opinion, Mr. President, David Hawk, the director of AXE, is selling these documents to the Russians. He has been doing it, as far as I can determine, for the last year and a half."

The President sat down in his chair and turned away so that he could look out the French doors at the Rose Garden.

"Mr. President," Mandel said, "something will have to be done—and soon."

NICK CARTER IS IT!

FROM THE NICK CARTER
KILLMASTER SERIES

AND NEXT THE KING
CHECKMATE IN RIO
THE COYOTE CONNECTION
THE DAY OF THE DINGO
DEATH MISSION: HAVANA
DOOMSDAY SPORE
EIGHTH CARD STUD
THE GALLAGHER PLOT
THE JUDAS SPY
THE MAN WHO SOLD DEATH
THE NICHOVEV PLOT
PAMPLONA AFFAIR
THE PEMEX CHART
THE Q MAN
THE REDOLMO AFFAIR
THE SATAN TRAP
THE SIGN OF THE PRAYER SHAWL
SIX BLOODY SUMMER DAYS
SOCIETY OF NINE
STRIKE OF THE HAWK
SUICIDE SEAT
TARANTULA STRIKE
TEMPLE OF FEAR
TEN TIMES DYNAMITE
THUNDERSTRIKE IN SYRIA
TIME CLOCK OF DEATH
TRIPLE CROSS
TURKISH BLOODBATH
TYPHOON RAY
UNDER THE WALL
WAR FROM THE CLOUDS
THE WEAPON OF NIGHT

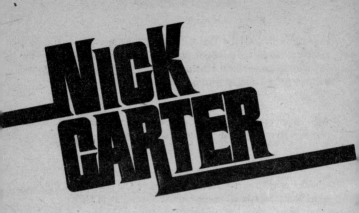

NICK CARTER

THE OUSTER CONSPIRACY

CHARTER
NEW YORK

A DIVISION OF CHARTER COMMUNICATIONS INC.
A GROSSET & DUNLAP COMPANY

THE OUSTER CONSPIRACY

A Charter Original.

First Charter Printing May 1981
Published simultaneously in Canada
Manufactured in the United States of America

2 4 6 8 0 9 7 5 3 1

PROLOGUE

A short, stoop-shouldered little man wearing a gray homburg and carrying a thick briefcase emerged from the Amalgamated Press building on Dupont Circle and climbed in the back seat of a waiting black Cadillac limousine, joining Air Force General Stewart LeMans.

When the driver had closed the rear door, he hurried around to the front, climbed in behind the wheel and pulled away from the curb, expertly merging with traffic.

For the first few moments neither man said anything, until General LeMans turned to look out the rear window. "We've got a tail."

"It's ours," the little man informed him. "Security."

LeMans looked at him. "Are you certain of your facts, Herbert? Dead certain?"

Herbert Mandel, chief administrative assistant to the director of AXE, the United States' most secret action service, nodded his head slightly, a pinched, disapproving expression coming across his thin lips. "Perfectly," he said. "But despite what you're probably thinking, it gives me absolutely no pleasure, LeMans."

"Christ," the general mumbled, slumping back in the deeply cushioned seat. "It's hard to believe."

The Cadillac had cut down Connecticut Avenue and as it approached Lafayette Square, Mandel tapped his briefcase with one bony finger. "There are going to be a great many people who'll find this hard to believe," he said.

"Who knows besides us?" the general asked. He was assigned as USAF advisor to NATO, and had just returned to Washington yesterday morning when Mandel had broken the news to him.

"No one," Mandel said. "I wanted to bring this personally to the President's attention before I went further."

"No word has been heard from him?"

"Not a thing," Mandel said. "But I've been seeing all the clues over the past few months. I even questioned him about it six weeks ago."

The general shook his head, still having difficulty in believing what he was hearing. "Which probably caused him to jump."

"Exactly," Mandel agreed.

The driver had turned the corner onto Pennsylvania Avenue, drove halfway down the block, then cut into the White House main gate, stopping smoothly at the guardhouse. Their security tail proceeded down the block and turned the corner.

Mandel lowered the window, as the guard approached the car, and held up his credentials. "The President is expecting us."

"Yes sir," the guard said. A moment later the iron gate swung open and they proceeded up the circular driveway.

They were shown immediately to the Oval Office where Mandel opened his briefcase and spread out a dozen documents, all marked "Top Secret: Limited NATO Distribution," on the President's desk.

"This is the latest batch, Mr. President," Mandel said. "They're all in the 700 series, as you can see."

General LeMans, who had not known exactly what to expect, was speechless for a moment.

"Do you recognize these general?" the President asked.

The general looked up and nodded. "Yes sir, Mr. President, I do, God help me."

The President turned to Mandel. "They're Category Q documents, aren't they?"

"Yes sir," Mandel said.

"And where were they found?"

"On the body of a KGB courier in Paris," Mandel said. He reached down and flipped several of the files open to the signature blocks.

The President followed the motion with his eyes, then shook his head. "Exactly what are you saying Mandel?"

Mandel looked from the President to LeMans, then back to the President. "In my opinion, Mr. President, David Hawk, the director of AXE, is selling these documents to the Russians. He has been doing it, as far as I can determine, for the last year and a half."

The President sat down in his chair and turned away so that he could look out the French doors at his Rose Garden.

"Mr. President," Mandel said, "something will have to be done—and soon."

ONE

"We'll be arriving at Washington's National Airport in just a few minutes. Please observe the no smoking and fasten seat belt signs, and thank you for flying Southern Airways. We hope your stay in Washington is a pleasant one," the stewardess said into the microphone from where she stood at the head of the main cabin.

I stubbed out my cigarette in the tiny armrest ashtray and laid my head back, going over in my mind one last time just how I was going to break the news to Hawk. He was not going to take it well; of that much I was sure. But just what he would say or do was a matter for great conjecture.

The office wags would probably have a field day with the bombshell I was going to drop on AXE headquarters. A number of them would be convinced that I had gone round the bend, that I had lost my nerve. A few others would be convinced that I was quitting because I didn't want to pull Duty Desk assignment. Still others would be certain that there had been some kind of a rift between Hawk and myself.

None of the above was true, of course, but the conjectures would race through the office like a prairie fire through Kansas in August.

I certainly was not going to enjoy my stay in Washington, contrary to the stewardess's best wishes. Nor had I enjoyed the Southern Airways flight. I haven't enjoyed commercial airline travel since the advent of airport security measures which have forced me to place my weapons in my luggage. Traveling without them was unsettling at best.

Over the past six weeks I had done a lot of thinking about myself, about AXE and its director, David Hawk, as well as Kazuka Akiyama, a girl I knew in Tokyo.

She had been engaged to my best friend Owen Nashima, AXE's director of Far East Operations, but a few years back he had been murdered. During the investigation into his death, Kazuka and I had fallen in love.

A lot of water had flowed under the bridge since that time; I had met and made love with a number of women, but always in the back of my mind was Kazuka.

Lovely Kazuka. I could see clearly in my mind's eye at this moment the pretty little Shinto temple outside her uncle's home in the mountains. We had spent five glorious days there, exploring each other's bodies as well as minds.

One week ago I had telephoned her where she worked as chief of station for AXE in Tokyo, told her I loved her—something I've rarely told any woman truthfully—and asked her to marry me.

"One condition Nick," she said, her voice intent.

"Anything," I said, raising my voice so that she could hear me plainly over the hiss and static of the international phone lines.

"Both of us will get out of the business."

For just a moment I had been stunned. But just for a moment. And then what she said seemed to make perfect sense. I had been around the world a hundred times. I had been wounded, more than once critically. And I had killed more people than I care to remember.

A year or so ago an AXE doctor had told me that my X-rays looked like a close up picture of a big bowl of spaghetti. I had joked with him, and asked how long I could expect to live if I got out of the business.

But he had not been amused, although he had laughed. "Carter," he said to me, "you have no life expectancy. You should be dead right now."

The doctor had X-rayed my body and had found it a mess. A year later Kazuka had X-rayed my soul and found it equally wanting.

I had not given her an answer on the phone that day, but agreed to give the matter a lot of thought.

Get out of AXE? It had been my life, one part of my brain said. Get out of AXE? It made perfect sense, another part of me argued.

Lovely Kazuka, I thought, but instead of her image, Hawk's face came into my mind's eyes.

"If that's what you want Carter—if that's what you really want—then get out, you're not the man I thought you were," Hawk's image said to me, and I began to sweat.

The DC 9 touched down, its tires barking against the pavement, and I opened my eyes, the same question that had plagued me for the past seven days rising up again.

How badly did I want Kazuka? Badly enough to give up my career as N3 Killmaster for AXE? Badly enough to incur the displeasure and maybe even disgust of Hawk, a man I trusted and loved? And if Kazuka could impose this kind of a condition on me now, what other conditions would she restrict me to later?

The turbine blades on the jet's huge engines reversed with a tremendous surge of power and the big aircraft screamed down the runway, its speed bleeding off until it slowly turned onto the taxiway and rumbled toward the terminal bulding.

I unfastened my seat belt, stood up in the aisle and retrieved my coat from the overhead locker under the disapproving scowl of one of the stewardesses. I looked her way, smiled and winked, and a startled expression crossed her features.

By the time I had slipped on my coat and worked my way to the forward door, the aircraft had turned into its terminal spot and the engines were whining down. Already the enclosed passenger ramp had snaked out to the forward door, and a stewardess was ready at the latch.

A moment later, the hatch was opened and I left the aircraft, brushing past a startled ground-crew member, deciding once and for all that I was going directly to see Hawk before I did anything else. I wanted to get it over with.

The boarding corridor twisted to the left, and then opened onto the Southern Airways gate area that was filled with passengers waiting to board once the plane was unloaded.

I was thinking about Hawk and exactly how I was going to break the news to him, so I didn't pay much attention to my surroundings as I strode through the boarding area and turned down the long, wide corridor which led to the baggage claim area. Otherwise I would have seen the large man carrying the ornately carved walking stick break away from the crowd and rapidly head my way.

At the same time, one of the stewardesses from my flight was running after me, the book I had been reading clutched in her hand.

"Mr. Carter," she was shouting. "Mr. Carter!"

I turned to see what the commotion was all about just as she collided with the man carrying the cane, only it wasn't a cane now—it was a long, deadly sword.

The man tried to push the startled girl out of his way, but she stumbled toward him. Whether he misread her intentions or not, I'll never know, because in the next instant he had run her through with the blade.

"Carter . . ." she said, as she slumped to the floor.

The man turned and headed down the corridor like a bolt of lightning. As I started after him, a dozen people surged from the boarding area to see what had happened, spilling out into the corridor, and I clashed with an old, incredibly fat woman. The two of us went down in a tangle of arms and legs and packages wrapped in brown paper.

By the time I had extricated myself the man with the cane had disappeared. I knew there would be no use in trying to find him in the crowded terminal, so I turned and went back to the stewardess.

One of the airline ticket agents had rushed to the fallen girl and had cradled her head in his arms.

"Susan," he was saying. "My God. *Susan*." He

looked up at me, tears streaming down his cheeks, and he shook his head. "Why?" he implored. "Why, did he do that?"

Even from where I stood I could see that the young woman was dead; the blade had evidently pierced her heart. And I knew another thing: The man with the cane had not come to the airport to kill a pretty stewardess. He had been after me, and except for the poor dumb misfortune of the girl running after me, I might be the one laying on the floor.

A number of passengers who had been waiting at the boarding gate had evidently come to the same conclusion, because they were staring at me with a mixture of open curiosity and fear.

Very quickly the police would be on the scene, and I did not want to go through the rigamarole that would entail, so I turned and nonchalantly walked away. I've learned over the years that ordinary people faced with extraordinary situations will do absolutely nothing until they have had enough time to sort out just what it was they had witnessed.

As I suspected, no alarm was sounded, no one challenged me, and by the time the police arrived the witnesses would give at least a half a dozen totally different descriptions of me and of the man with the cane.

But I had seen the man clearly for just that moment before he turned and hurried away. He had a face I would never forget. His features were thick and dark; I had noticed the heavy eyebrows and deep-set eyes. Baltic. Perhaps Hungarian or East German, possibly even European Russian.

I had plenty of enemies in those places, but why try to assassinate me now, here at the Washington airport, unless something was coming up? Some assignment was in the offing that the opposition did not want me to take?

Two police officers rushed by me, one of them frantically speaking into a walkie-talkie. A moment later I passed the boarding area security station and took the escalator down to the street level.

Halfway down I took off my tie, pulled off my jacket, draping it casually over my arm, and put on a pair of sunglasses. The slight change in my appearance would assure me enough time to claim my luggage and then catch a cab for town, even if one of the witnesses could give the police an accurate description of me.

I stepped off the escalator and spotted Hawk's assistant, Herbert Mandel, turning away from an airport security man. When he saw me he beckoned and came my way.

Mandel had worked with AXE for the last ten years, coming, as far as I knew, out of Harvard as one of Henry Kissinger's cronies, if not friends. For a time he had lorded over Personnel and Pay, later Procedures, and finally became assistant chief of operations—number two behind Hawk.

I had never particularly disliked Mandel, although I never liked him either; I suppose my neutrality came from the days when he was head of Personnel and Pay, and he and I had had words on more than one occasion over my somewhat unorthodox expenditures of AXE funds.

There was always something about Mandel, however, that I found disquieting, and for the life of me I've never been able to figure out why Hawk had made him his assistant. Of course I never voiced those opinions to Hawk, it wasn't my place.

Mandel finally reached me and stuck out his hand. "Welcome back, Carter. Hope you had a pleasant flight."

I wanted to ask him what he was doing greeting me at the airport, but instead I nodded. "Not bad except for the fact that someone just tried to kill me."

Mandel's complexion turned a pasty color, and he looked over my shoulder.

"He's gone," I said. "Killed a young stewardess who got in the way. I'll work up an Identa-Kit on him as soon as we get back to the office. I'd like to nail the bastard. Is there anything going on that I should know about?"

It was then that I noticed the strange, pinched expression on the man's face.

"Plenty," he said. "But we'd better get out of here. My car is out front. Your baggage will be sent along."

He turned without another word and shuffled toward the main doors. I followed him, a funny feeling starting up in my gut. Something was going on, and I expected I was not going to like it very much.

"What do you know about NATO?" Mandel asked when we had settled into the back seat of his limousine and the driver had pulled away from the curb.

I raised my eyebrows slightly. We were going to play twenty questions about whatever my assignment was going to be. Already, however, I knew it was big. Someone had sent a hit man to meet me at the airport, and here was AXE's number two man giving me a ride into town.

"North Atlantic Treaty Organization," I answered. "Formed in forty-eight or forty-nine I think."

"Forty-nine," Mandel said.

"Bob Burns is our liaison over there in intelligence. I worked with him a few years back. Good man."

Mandel nodded after each point. "How about the organization? What do you know about that?"

"Not a lot," I said, trying to figure out what this was all about. "The top brass make up what is called the North Atlantic Council. Under them are the NATO Secretary General, his staff and then the Military Committee. Below that I couldn't tell you much."

"And NATO Series documents?" he asked.

I shrugged. "The one hundreds deal with Communist Bloc cooperation. The two hundreds, with Communist Bloc troop distribution—"

"The Series 700," he interrupted.

My gut flopped over, and I really looked at Mandel this time. There was a thin bead of sweat forming on his upper lip. "The most important of all," I said. "Lower seven hundreds deal with NATO's nuclear strike capabilities, and the upper levels deal with the member nations' ability to withstand a nuclear attack."

"Indeed," Mandel said. "Distribution?"

"To member nations. Heads of state."

"How about U.S. distribution?"

My gut flopped again. "The President to start with; I think they're all Category Q aren't they?"

Mandel nodded.

"Then Cat Q starts with the President and includes the Joint Chiefs, Secretary of Defense, Secretary of State, the heads of the CIA and AXE, and, I think, the National Security Adviser as well as our representative on the NATO Military Committee."

Mandel nodded again, and it was then that I noticed we had not turned north on Twenty-third Street after the

Arlington Memorial Bridge which would take us to the
office. Instead, the chauffeur had turned up Bacon
Drive and then east on Constitution.

"Where are we going?" I asked.

"The White House," Mandel answered softly.
"The President would like to speak to you."

"Jesus," I said, and sat back in the deeply cushioned
seat. I pulled a cigarette from my pocket, lit it and
inhaled deeply as I tried to think this out. Whatever was
happening *was* big, much bigger than I had first suspected.

Evidently something was going on with NATO
Series 700 documents, which were the most closely
guarded of all the organization's secrets. Even the mere
knowledge of their existence was classified Top Secret.

I knew it would do no good for me to ask Mandel
what was going on. If he had wanted to tell me he would
be doing so right now.

The President was seated in his position at the large
conference table in the Cabinet meeting room. To his
right and left were his National Security Adviser, the
head of the Joint Chiefs, the Secretary of Defense and
the Secretary of State.

Directly across from the President was Admiral Wal-
ter Haiger, head of the Central Intelligence Agency,
and to his left Air Force General Stewart LeMans.
There were two empty chairs to Haiger's right, which
he motioned for us to take.

"How much have you told him already, Herbert?"
the President asked softly.

"Nothing, Mr. President, I merely questioned him
on his knowledge of NATO and the Series documents."

"I don't know what this is all about, Mr. President," I broke in. "But I believe you should be made aware of the fact that someone attempted to kill me at the airport as I got off the plane."

Everyone looked startled except for Mandel who already knew, and the President who seemed definitely worried by the news.

"Did he know Carter was scheduled in?" the President asked Mandel.

"There's no question of it, Mr. President."

"Good Lord," the President said sitting back in his chair.

"A group of Series 700 documents were discovered on the body of a dead KGB courier in Paris thirty-six hours ago," the President began. "The man was hit by a car, evidently on his way to Orly Field. He had reservations for an Air Finland flight to Helsinki. From there he would have made it across the border. We had no inkling of what was happening there. None whatsoever."

"Someone is selling the Russians NATO documents," I said. My hands were cold.

The President nodded. "As far as Mr. Mandel can determine it has been going on now for the better part of a year and a half."

"You want me to find out who?" I asked, but the President shook his head.

"We know who," he said. "This man is in hiding."

"Who is he?" I asked softly.

The President took a long time to answer. When he finally did, his manner was hesitant, which was very unsettling to witness in a President.

"There is incontrovertible evidence that David Hawk has been selling NATO Series 700 documents to the Soviets. Mr. Mandel has suspected for some time, and twelve hours ago Hawk disappeared.''

The room seemed to be tilting and spinning around me, and although the President was still talking—something about Mandel coming to him so that there would be no questions of rivalry or some inner office plot to dethrone Hawk—I was not really listening. My entire world had just been turned upside down, and it was going to take me a while to straighten it out again.

TWO

"Who in the office besides you and me knows about this?" I asked, finally getting my voice. We had left the Cabinet room shortly after two o'clock, and had gone directly outside where Mandel's driver was waiting with the limousine.

The day was still bright and warm under a cloudless sky, but for me it seemed as if a cold wind was blowing directly from the Arctic.

"No one," he said getting in the back seat. "We're going to keep it that way too, Carter, at least for now."

"What's the official line?"

Mandel looked at me, his eyes blinking, but before he answered he flipped the switch that raised a transparent but soundproof glass barrier between us and the driver. "There is no line. He's in the field, that's all."

I looked away, still not able to assign any reality to what I had learned, let alone even come close to believing it. Hawk was no more of a traitor than I was, although at this moment I was definitely having traitorous thoughts.

Mandel must have read my mind. "You saw the documents yourself, Carter. Hawk's signature was on every one of them."

I turned back. "How do you know they weren't forgeries?"

"The lab people verified his signature from other documents he had signed."

"I thought you said no one else knew about this."

"We lifted the signatures off the documents, then gave them to the lab people as an exercise. Pick up the fake. They couldn't. They were all real."

"What am I supposed to do?" I asked. "Wring a confession out of him? Torture perhaps?"

"Kill him," Mandel said softly.

For a moment I wasn't sure I had heard him correctly, but he continued, erasing all doubt from my mind.

"If you brought him in and he did confess, which is highly unlikely, it would tear the service apart. There could be no public trial of course, but still there would be repercussions."

"You're asking me to kill a man I've worked for nearly all my adult life?"

"Robert Burns has come over from Geneva to help out. If you can't pull the trigger he will."

"I'm to lead him to Hawk, then?" I said, my voice rising.

"Come on Carter, you've had the N3 Killmaster designation for a number of years now. You're a professional. You've been on other nasty assignments. If you don't want the job any longer we can pull your N3 and assign you somewhere else.''

He had half turned in his seat so that he was directly facing me. ''You're the only one who can do this job. You know him better than any of us. You know his habits, his likes, his dislikes. I've put out a few feelers on my own, of course, but I've come up with a complete blank. He's too good.''

''The best,'' I said absently.

''If anyone can find him it'll be you. And it has to be done, make no mistake about it.''

I started to argue with him, but he cut me off.

''Listen to me Carter—with your brain not your emotions. Think of what's happening here. We're talking about Series 700 documents. He's got another batch with him. Recent assessments of our own nuclear strike capabilities. And they don't paint a very rosy picture. If ever there was a time for the opposition to attack it's right now.''

''How do you know it's not already too late?'' I asked. ''Maybe he's already out of the country. Maybe he's already passed on the documents.'' I could not believe I was saying the things I was.

''We don't,'' Mandel admitted. ''It's another of the reasons we want you and Burns to work together. You must find him and fast.''

We rode the rest of the way to my apartment in Chevy Chase in silence. Only after the car stopped and I opened the door to get out, did Mandel speak up.

''Burns should be coming to your place within the hour. You'll have an unlimited budget on this one, with no time frame other than most immediate.''

''How about my things?''

''Already upstairs,'' Mandel said as the car began to

slide away from the curb. "Good luck."

For some odd reason I got the impression that he really didn't mean it. Perhaps like me he did not believe Hawk was guilty, and yet he had been forced by virtue of his position to issue the orders he had.

I watched until the car disappeared around the corner before going up to my apartment. Inside the air was stuffy; it had been a half a dozen weeks since I had been home.

My suitcase was sitting in the middle of the living room floor. I went across the room, picked it up and went tiredly into my bedroom where Bob Burns was sitting propped up in my bed reading a magazine. He was dressed in a European cut, dove gray suit, with well shined, low-top dress boots. He looked natty.

"Sorry old top," he said softly. "But I don't think they quite trust you on this one."

I crossed the room and flopped my suitcase on the bed, then opened it, extracting the leather case that contained the three weapons I always carry: my 9 mm Luger, my stiletto with its chamois case, and Pierre, my gas bomb which fits in a specially built pouch strapped to my leg, almost like a third testicle.

"When were you told about it?" I asked nonchalantly over my shoulder as I went into the bathroom.

"Last night," came the reply.

I quickly strapped my weapons on, making sure my Luger, Wilhelmina, was loaded, and, feeling much better about everything, went back into the bedroom. "Trust me or not, Bob, I'm working alone on this one," I said evenly.

Burns started to reach inside his coat, but I had my Luger out first, snapped the slide back, injecting a live round into the chamber, and pointed it at his head.

"Alone, Bob," I said. "And I think you know I mean it."

For a long moment Burns's right hand remained in his coat, but then he pulled it out very slowly and empty, then shrugged. "You're calling the shots for the moment."

"What are your orders?" I asked.

"Stick with you until we find Hawk."

"And then?"

"Kill him if you can't, or won't."

"And if I refuse to cooperate with you?"

Burns carefully raised his left hand and rubbed at his left eyebrow. He seemed suddenly very nervous.

I took a step closer to the bed. "If I refuse to cooperate with you, what then Bob? What are your orders?"

"I'm to assume, in that case, that you're either in sympathy with Hawk, or in league with him."

"In which case you'd have to kill me."

Burns nodded. "I'm afraid so."

"There's a fail-safe out there I imagine," I said, nodding toward the front door.

"Three sets actually. A pair out front and a pair out back. The third I believe is on the roof."

"Any idea where Hawk jumped to?"

"None," Burns said. "We were hoping you could supply that information. We're pretty certain he hasn't made it out of the country—at least not by any normal means."

That was all I needed to hear. I knew where he was. And I had a pretty fair idea that he was waiting for me to show up. *Alone*.

"What about the people downstairs," I asked. "What have they been told?"

"Nothing about Hawk," Burns said, seeming even

more nervous. "As far as they're concerned you and I are working together on something that was set up to test your loyalty. If you try to jump they've got orders to nail you."

"All right," I said. "We're getting out of here. I think I know where he is."

Burns' face lit up and he started to sit forward but I waved him back.

"Unbutton your coat," I said. "Carefully."

For a moment a look of confusion clouded his expression, but then understanding dawned in his eyes, which narrowed a moment later.

"Don't try it Bob," I said. "You're a good man, and I like you. Don't blow it with heroics."

At first it looked as if he was going to ignore my advice, but then he let out a deep breath, managed a slight grin and very carefully unbuttoned his suit jacket to reveal a .38 Police Special in a thick, regulation holster. Burns had no imagination.

"I want the gun on the bed, and I want you on your feet. Slowly," I said.

Burns complied, his every motion deliberate. "You won't get out of here without me," he said. "And I'm not coming with you."

"I know," I said. "But I want you to step away from the bed and then go out into the living room."

"Whatever you say, Nick," he said as he moved toward the door. "But the living room is as far as I'm going."

"It's all right," I said, pocketing his gun and following him into the other room where I motioned him to sit in one of the easy chairs. When he had settled down, I went to the window, eased the curtain back and peered down to the street. Two men were seated in a plain blue sedan, watching my building.

Burns did not move from his seat as I went around the room turning on all the lights, but he watched me with open curiosity.

Next I went to the door, which I unlocked, then back to the window where I drew the curtains open. One of the men in the surveillance car was looking up at the window as I moved away from it to a low table nearby.

"What are you doing?" Burns asked.

"You'll see," I said, picking up the lamp that was on the table. In one smooth motion, I turned on my heel and threw it at the window. The glass shattered and the lamp went through.

"What the hell—" Burns started to shout, but I motioned him back to his chair and I took a seat on the couch facing the door.

"We've only got a minute now Bob, so I'm going to say this just once." Burns stared at me wide-eyed, his hands tightly gripping the arms of his chair. "I'm going to see Hawk. If he is a traitor I'll kill him myself. If he's not the one selling the documents to the Soviets, I'll find out who is."

Burns nodded but said nothing. A few seconds later we both could hear the pounding of feet outside in the corridor, and he stiffened.

"Warn them and I'll kill you," I said softly. I held my Luger in my right hand alongside my leg.

The door burst open and a man I was sure I had seen around AXE headquarters leaped inside, his gun drawn. His tie was loose and he needed a shave. I wondered how long he had been sitting waiting for me.

Neither Burns nor I said a thing, and the man stood stock still in the doorway, his eyes flitting from me to the broken window and back again.

"What the hell is going on in there?" someone called from the corridor.

"Beats me," the man in the doorway said, lowering his gun. "What's happening here Bob?" he asked.

Burns turned in his chair and looked up at him. I tensed. "Nick has something to say to you, I think."

"It's all right," the man in the doorway said, and a moment later his partner came around the corner and entered the room. He too had his weapon drawn, and in his left hand he held a walkie-talkie.

"Tell them to stand down," I said calmly. "I've got something to tell you."

The second man held the walkie-talkie up to his lips without hesitation and pushed the transmit button. "Units two and three, clear. It's a false alarm. Stand down and return to your positions."

Both men came all the way into the living room, closed the door behind them and holstered their weapons.

"Now what the hell is—" one of them started to say when I raised my Luger.

"Put the walkie-talkie down," I cut him off. "Push the transmit button and you're a dead man."

"Bob—" he started to say, but again I interrupted him.

"Put the walkie-talkie down on the floor and step away from it. *Now!*"

"Better do as he says," Burns advised, and the man complied.

I got up from where I was sitting on the couch and moved away from it, keeping my Luger trained on both men.

"One at a time now, I want you to carefully take your weapons out and lay them on the floor. Then come over here by the couch and lay face-down on the floor, your hands behind your back and your legs crossed."

If they had simply said no, I don't know what I would

have done. I could not have shot them; they were not the enemy. But they did as I said, finally, and when they were down, I scooped up their weapons as well as the walkie-talkie.

Quickly I ducked into my bedroom and grabbed my suitcase. In the few seconds it took me Burns had nearly made it to the door.

"Don't," I snapped. "Back on the floor, Bob. If you come after me I'll shoot to kill."

Sheepishly Burns came back across the room and laid down. A moment later I was out in the corridor taking the stairs down two at a time to the first floor.

It would not take them very long to alert their teams out back and on the roof, nor would it take them very long to call for reinforcements, but I didn't need much time.

Within minutes, I was behind the wheel of the surveillance car, had driven around the corner and had abandoned the car on a back street. I walked up to Dorset Avenue in Somerset Heights where I hailed a passing cab.

"The airport," I said, sitting back in the seat and trying to think this thing out.

NATO documents with Hawk's signature on them had been found on a Russian courier. If Hawk hadn't sent them over, who had? And how had they come up with the documents in the first place?

As hard as I tried, I could not think of any possible way for it to happen without Hawk knowing, and I began to get seriously worried.

David Hawk was waiting for me at his cabin on Little Moose Lake in the Adirondacks eighty miles northwest of Albany, New York.

It was late afternoon of the next day and I was dead tired. I had driven all night from the Washington airport, my mind a seething cauldron of conjecture, doubt and disbelief. Hawk was not a traitor. And yet he had jumped. Why?

A couple of years ago, in one of his rare, chatty moods, he had confided in me that several years before he had purchased a small fishing cabin on the northern New York lake: ''For the day that I get tired of all this and decide to bail out,'' he had said.

He had described the cabin to me in loving detail, including the complicated directions for finding it. And he had also told me that no other living soul knew about it. He had purchased the place through a series of blind real estate trust accounts in a number of different names. There was absolutely no way of tracing its ownership to him.

I would never have remembered the conversation or anything about the cabin, except for the fact that at the time it had struck me as very odd that Hawk would ever consider ''bailing out,'' as he called it.

He was down by a rickety old wooden dock that jutted a hundred feet out into the lake, fishing pole in hand, when I came up the driveway and parked in front of the cabin. When I got out of the car he motioned for me to join him.

After the warm humid weather of Washington, the weather here in the mountains was refreshingly cool and clear. A pleasant change.

''How's the fishing, sir,'' I said as I stepped off the shore and onto the dock. He was seated at the end, and he turned to me. The stub of a long dead cigar was clenched firmly in his mouth, but there was no smile on his lips.

"Lousy," he grumbled. "Did you cover your tracks?"

"Yes sir," I said finally reaching him. I squatted down on my haunches and lit myself a cigarette. My hands were shaking. I didn't want him to be guilty. Not him. "Bought airline tickets on three major airlines for three different destinations under three of my usual aliases. Then rented a car under my real name with the stated destination as Miami, Florida. I had the Sheraton downtown make reservations for me in Tampa."

"No one tailed you out of the city?"

I shook my head, a little hurt that Hawk would question my tradecraft. "No sir. I'm clean."

Hawk looked deeply into my eyes for a long moment before he turned away to stare out across the lake to the opposite shore where pine trees grew thick to the water's edge. When he spoke again there was a weariness in his voice that I had never heard before. It made me even more nervous.

"First," he growled, "I'm not the traitor that Mandel thinks I am. I have not sold the Russians or anyone else NATO documents."

It was like a cold drink of water on a hot day for a man dying of thirst. "I'm glad to hear that, sir. Very glad."

Hawk looked at me sharply. "What'd they tell you?"

Quickly I recounted for him everything that Mandel had told me, and then my briefing with the President in the Cabinet room as well as Bob Burns's involvement.

"Mandel told you to kill me?"

I nodded.

"Good man," he snarled. "If our positions had been

reversed, I would have given the same orders. For the good of the service.''

I didn't say a thing.

"You're leaving something out. What else happened?"

"Someone came after me in the airport when I flew in from Phoenix," I said, explaining what had happened, including a description of the man with the cane.

"No time for an Identa-Kit drawing I suppose?"

"No sir."

Hawk fell silent for a moment, and I could almost hear the gears clicking in his brain. When he looked up he seemed particularly grim, and about twenty years older.

"You're going to be working on your own on this one, Nick, that is if you're taking the assignment. There'll be no agency backing."

"I'm taking it," I said.

Hawk nodded. "Mandel came to me a few weeks ago with his questions about the Series 700 documents," he began. "As far as I could see, reading between his lines, I felt that he had at least a *prima facie* case against me and it looked as if he was going to push it."

"So you jumped," I said.

"So I jumped," Hawk agreed. "I took with me the last batch of seven hundreds. If there's a Cat Q leak in our office I didn't want the documents to continue being piped over. If the leak is elsewhere it'll show up soon."

"I don't understand why you jumped, sir. Why didn't you stay and fight it?"

"The files I took out of my office safe—the Series 700s—all bear my signature," he said carefully.

"Only it isn't my signature."

"What?" I asked confused.

"I signed during distribution, but the files in my safe are not the ones I signed."

"Who has your safe combination besides you?" I asked. "Mandel?"

"No one," Hawk said. "And my safe has not been tampered with."

"How then—" I started to ask, but he held me off.

"The routine is for me to go to Geneva twice a year, sign for the documents, then bring them back with me. Somewhere over there, somehow, fakes with my forged signatures were switched. Of course I never look at my signature once I've signed. No need to. Apparently this has been going on for some time."

"But why?" I asked. "It doesn't make any sense. Why go through all that trouble if whoever is doing this has the unsigned documents in the first place?"

"Someone in NATO evidently wants my hide, wants me out of AXE. They've got NATO documents bearing my legitimate signature which they're passing on to the Russians. Or perhaps even the Russians were duped. Perhaps the documents they found on the dead courier in Paris were the first batch. Perhaps they gave him the files with my signature and then killed him."

"Christ," I said, running the fingers of my right hand through my hair.

"That's an understatement," Hawk said. "It's an ouster conspiracy to get rid of me—at least I hope that's all it is. But it's a can of worms. I'm a traitor as far as my own service is concerned, and now by association so are you. Which means you'll be totally on your own from this point on, with half the world trying to find and kill you."

THREE

North Springfield is not the most exclusive of Washington, D.C. suburbs; but it is a quiet one, especially at four in the morning.

I parked my car around the corner from the Carlton Arms Singles apartment complex on Braddock Road and went the rest of the way on foot, just in case Mandel's unlimited budget now included me. The key to the puzzle, I was fairly certain, lay in Brussels, Belgium, in or around NATO headquarters. But first there were a couple of answers and some help I needed here.

Sandry Triggs, who worked in Archives, was the Home Station's chief artist. She and I had had a thing together a few years ago and ever since then she had been trying for a repeat performance.

Almost even more importantly for me at the moment, was the fact that Sandry was, hands down, the office's chief gossip. She had told me with pride on more than one occasion that her ears were firmly planted in the office grapevine, and if only she could plant her butt just as firmly in my bed she'd be the happiest woman alive.

On top of all that she was good looking.

A plain gray sedan with government plates was parked in front of Sandry's apartment building, and even in the darkness I could see the outlines of two men in the front seat.

The rest of the street was deserted except a half a block away, on the opposite side, where someone was getting gasoline at an all night station.

They hadn't waited very long to decide that I had skipped, and to stopper up all my contacts. Washington, from this moment on, was going to be a tough town to maneuver in.

It would slow me down by a dozen hours or so, but it really didn't matter. Hawk was safe for the time being at his cabin, and I desperately needed the rest.

I hurried back around the corner to where I had parked the rental car and drove three blocks away where I found a phone booth a half a block up from a parking ramp. It was exactly what I wanted.

I drove to the highest level of the nearly deserted ramp, and parked in a slot with a twenty-four hour meter which I plugged. I carefully wiped away all my fingerprints and cleaned the ashtray of my cigarette butts, in case I could not get back here for some reason, then I hurried down to the street.

A police car cruised slowly by as I stood in the shadows. When it was gone, I hurried the rest of the way down the street to the phone booth. Once inside I left the door half ajar so the light wouldn't come on and dialed Sandry's number.

Her phone would be tapped, I was sure, but it would not matter providing she would cooperate quickly enough so I could keep the call short, and therefore trace-proof.

On the fourth ring her sleepy voice answered, "Yes? Who is it?"

"It's me, sweetheart," I said lightly, and she was instantly awake.

"Oh boy, are you in hot—" she started, but then bit off the words.

"I need your help," I said tersely.

"You got it, if I can manage."

"Jump in your car and drive down to the Washington monument."

"Right now . . . this morning?" she asked.

"Right now," I said. "If you're clean I'll make contact."

"If I'm not?"

"Try again in twelve hours. Same routine."

"On my way," she said, and she hung up. She was one of the good ones.

I left the phone booth and quickly made my way on foot the three blocks toward her apartment building where I walked into the all night gas station, got some change and bought a pack of cigarettes from the vending machine.

Sandry's car, a dark blue Mustang II, came from behind the apartment building at high speed and screamed down the street toward town, the surveillance car starting up and chasing after her.

When they were out of sight, I thanked the sleepy attendant, crossed the street and entered the apartment building, going immediately to the fifth floor where I ducked into the stairwell down the corridor from her door.

I needed Sandry's help but I didn't want to get her too deeply into trouble. When this was over and I was away, I'd telephone her and tell her that she was being tailed and thanks anyway for the help.

It would cover her, although she would get reamed by Mandel for not reporting my first call.

The elevator indicator showed that someone was coming up from the garage level and I stiffened. Nearly two hours had elapsed since Sandry had left. She had been due back long ago, unless she had taken a dozen or more turns around the Washington Monument.

The elevator doors slid open finally, and Sandry stepped out. She headed slowly down the corridor to her apartment door, and I could see that she was tired, and disappointed.

No one else had called for the elevator, nor could I hear anyone on the stairwell below me. The surveillance team had probably taken up station again outside, accepting my call and rendezvous instructions at face value. When this was all over and Hawk was again back in the saddle, I was going to write a long memo on the lack of imagination in field men.

Just before she got to her apartment door I stepped out of the stairwell, and her eyes nearly popped out of their sockets. I motioned for her to keep silent just as she was about to shout my name. She instantly understood and waited for me to get to her.

She was dressed in tight jeans, sneakers and a thin cotton blouse that left absolutely no question she had gone without a bra. Her hair was a mess, but she looked stunning.

When I reached her, I drew her away from her apartment door. "There's a tap on your phone and your place is probably bugged."

A grim expression crossed her petite features. "They want you pretty badly. I saw the creeps following me."

"I want you to open your apartment door and go inside like nothing happened. Wash your hands and face or take a shower or something while I look around."

Her eyes had lit up as I spoke. "You staying long?"

"Until four this afternoon when you're going out for a second rendezvous try."

"Lovely," she said. "I'll call in sick. Since they've got a tap on my phone they'll expect it."

I nodded. She turned and went to her door and noisily unlocked it, sighing theatrically as she went inside, me silently behind her.

When she had her door re-locked and the chain on, she turned around and gave me a silent kiss, then headed for the bathroom, pulling her blouse off as she walked and tossing it on the couch.

At the bathroom door she turned and winked at me, the nipples on her lovely breasts already hard.

Ordinarily I don't like being cooped up for any reason. But I had a definite feeling that this was going to be one of the more pleasant twelve-hour periods of confinement I'd spent in a long time.

When she was in the bathroom running the shower, I quickly worked my way around the living room, checking lamps, pictures on the walls, door and window frames, finally finding a miniature bug behind one of the sofa cushions. I left it intact. It would not pick up anything from the bathroom or bedroom anyway.

In her bedroom, which was pink and frilly, I found a second bug behind the bureau mirror, the ultrasensitive microphone pointed directly at the bed. They had all the angles covered—all but one that is.

Carefully I leaned forward, puckered up my lips less than an inch away from the mike and blew as hard as I could. At the monitoring and recording end it would sound like a sudden burst of static and then nothing as the output sections of the tiny self-contained transmitter overloaded and burned out because of the sudden sharp increase in air pressure.

I didn't think they'd plant a bug in the bathroom, not with the living room and bedroom covered, but I went in quietly anyway, trying as hard as I could to avoid looking at Sandry's lovely body under the spray of the shower, and did a quick search, finding nothing.

When I was finished I closed the door and turned to face her. She had opened the shower door and was smiling at me.

"Are . . . we . . . clean?" she mouthed the words.

"Not as clean as you'll be when I finish washing your back," I said as I started to undress.

I was dreaming about Hawk. He was lying, unconscious on the desert floor far below me as I and dozens of other vultures circled overhead. I wanted to go down to help him, but I couldn't. The wings of the other birds kept getting in my way . . . brushing my face and my entire body with the soft feathers at their wingtips.

After a while I could hear their gentle cooing and smell their delicate feminine odor, and I came slowly awake.

Sandry was astraddle me, brushing my face and my chest with the tips of her breasts, and when I opened my eyes she smiled.

"A girl has to practically knock herself out to get any

attention from you,'' she said, pouting.

I kissed her breasts, then reached up and drew her down so that she was lying full length atop me. Her eyes closed, her mouth half opened and a moment later I was inside her, slowly, luxuriously making love.

It was the second time this morning we had made love, I thought when we were finished and she had rolled over on her side of the bed. She was tracing little light patterns on my chest with the fingertips of her right hand, when I held my left arm up to look at my watch. It read a few minutes before three.

For several seconds the luminous dials did not register on my brain, but when they finally did, I sat up with a start. It was nearly three! I had slept the entire morning and most of the afternoon.

Sandry was going to have to be out of here within the next forty minutes or so for our supposed second try at a rendezvous, and I had gotten none of the information I needed.

I reached over and gently kissed her on the lips, then rolled her half off the bed, slapping her sharply on the rump.

"Fun time is over," I said, swinging my legs over the opposite side of the bed and getting up. I grabbed my clothes and headed for the door but before I opened it I looked back at Sandry who had rolled back onto the bed and was watching me.

"Another twelve hours?" she asked petulantly.

I shook my head. "Have you got a sketch pad around here?"

She propped herself up on her elbows, a quizzical expression on her face. "Of course."

"Get it out," I said. "As soon as I take a shower we've got some work to do."

She seemed hurt. "Is that all you came to me for?"

I went back to the bed and looked down at her. "Listen to me, Sandry. Unless I miss my bet you have a fair idea of what's been happening over the past couple of days."

She nodded. "I think so."

"I've got to stop it, and not only for Hawk's sake."

Her eyes had gone wide, and she swallowed. "I don't understand Nick, but all right," she said. "I trust you."

I turned and softly let myself out of the bedroom and padded into the bathroom where I took a quick shower, shaved, using her razor, and got dressed. When I was finished I went back into the bedroom where she had already gotten dressed and was sitting in a chair by the window, her sketch pad in hand.

"Round face . . . square face . . . light . . . dark," she said.

I came up behind her. "Square face, heavy, dark features. Bulgarian or maybe European Russian," I said, and she began sketching, quickly and expertly.

As she worked I kept up a running commentary of facial characteristics and corrections to what she was doing, and within ten minutes Sandry had drawn me a reasonably accurate sketch of the man who had tried to kill me at the airport.

"That's him," I said when she had finished. She started to tear the sketch out of the book, but I stopped her. "I don't want it. I want you to take it back to work and put a name to it, along with some background."

She nodded. "How will I get the information to you?"

"I have a blind letter box in Paris. Madame Rochard's," I said, giving her the address of the small bistro. "As soon as you have anything express mail it to me there."

"What else?" she asked looking away.

I gently turned her face up toward mine. "Don't sell yourself short, Sandry," I said. "This has nothing to do with you, or what you and I have together. The service is in big trouble, and I'm going to do whatever it takes to straighten it out."

She sighed. "I guess I understand, Nick. I'm just being selfish."

"You're anything but that. When this is over with I'll come back and we'll work something out."

She brightened perceptibly.

"Now, what's the latest scuttlebutt around the office?" I asked.

She shrugged. "There hasn't been much, except that you're supposedly AWOL. They've pulled in all their legmen to run you down. Most of them are sure you're shacked up somewhere and will come out of the woods in good time."

"How about Hawk?"

Her eyes narrowed. "What do you mean?"

"What's the word about him?"

"I don't understand, Nick," she said. "As far as I know he's out on a field mission. Mandel is running the Ops Desk while he's gone."

"Anything else?" I asked.

She shook her head. "Should there be?"

I looked at my watch, ignoring her last question. It was twenty to four. "Time to go," I said. I bent down and kissed her. "And thanks, Sandry . . . for everything."

"My pleasure," she said with a lascivious grin.

The switchoff had gone fine: Sandry left in her Mustang II for our rendezvous, the surveillance car followed her and I simply walked the three blocks to the parking ramp where I retrieved my rental car.

Despite the easy departure, however, it was well after 6:00 P.M. before I cleared Washington, D.C., because of the traffic. Outside Baltimore I stopped at a shopping center where I bought a bottle of hair bleach, a toothbrush and, at an optometrist's shop, a pair of expensive sunglasses whose lenses would remain clear in the dark, making them appear as if they were normal prescription glasses.

Around eight I stopped again at a truck stop where I had a quick and lousy meal. Before leaving I telephoned Sandry to tell her that she was being followed and to thank her for her attempt to help me.

It was nearly one in the morning when I finally reached New York City, crossing into Manhattan over the George Washington Bridge. Making sure I had again cleaned off or smudged my fingerprints, I left the car unlocked just off Central Park East, and a block later dropped the keys down a sewer grate. Within a couple of hours the car would either be stripped or stolen. Either way it would take days for the police to trace it to the rental agency in Washington, D.C., and then back to me—if they ever did.

I took a cab downtown fo Forty-sixth Street, just off Broadway, and checked into a sleazy hotel. Twice during the night I almost went downstairs to the pay phone to call Kazuka, but both times I thought better of it, and instead sat by the window waiting for the gray dawn to come over the city.

Washington would be frantic by now, I figured. But they'd probably leave Sandry alone for at least another twenty-four hours against the possibility that I might try to contact her again. After that, however, it could get a little uncomfortable for her. I only hoped that she would have enough time to put some information to the sketch she had drawn and get it off to me in Paris.

Early the next morning I went looking for a used clothing store. Walking west for a few blocks, I finally found a small shop nestled between two run down apartment buildings. I purchased three old suits, several shirts, a couple of pairs of shoes and several gaudy ties.

At a nearby pawn shop I bought a battered old suitcase with travel stickers on it from a dozen countries, as well as a cheap 35 mm camera outfit complete with a scuffed carrying case.

I returned to the hotel and repacked my things in the old suitcase, then went down to the desk where I slipped the clerk a hundred dollar bill along with one week's room rent.

"I don't want to be disturbed for the next seven days, friend," I told the clerk whose eyes nearly popped out of their sockets at the sight of the money.

"Yes, sir," he stammered.

"In fact I'm not even here, am I? I never was here."

The clerk stared at me dumbfounded.

"It's nothing illegal," I said and winked.

"Of course, sir," the clerk answered grinning. "Of course."

Back in my room, I bleached my hair almost completely white, using the toothbrush to carefully work some of the coloring into my eyebrows. Next, I dressed in one of the old suits, knotting the colorful tie crookedly, and donned the clear sunglasses before I left via the fire escape.

Four blocks from the hotel there was a huge arcadelike store that sold cigarettes, posters, tee shirts and souvenirs on one side; the other side was filled with pinball machines. All the machines were in use and the noise was deafening. No one noticed me as I headed for the photo booth in the rear. I took four shots of myself for fifty cents.

Before sneaking back to the hotel, I stopped for coffee and a sandwich. While I waited for my order, I used the pay phone near the door to call for a reservation on the 8:00 P.M. flight to Paris.

Safe in my room again, I withdrew a blank passport from my documents kit, attached one of the photos and stamped my name as Albert Sutherland, with a birthdate making me in my late fifties.

Pierre, my gas bomb, I hid in the back of the 35mm camera. My stiletto snapped onto its specially constructed mounting, which made it look like some kind of a wall hanging complete with frame. And my Luger I completely disassembled, stuffing some of the parts in and among my camera equipment, other parts in my shaving kit and the handle inside a can of shaving cream.

I was ready—or at least as ready as I was going to be. But what would be waiting for me once I made it to Brussels, I couldn't even guess.

FOUR

Paris greeted me like it would any other apparently down at the heels visitor—with indifference. The customs inspector at Orly Field only gave my passport a cursory glance, and paid even less attention to my suitcase and camera bag, making his little chalk marks on my luggage with the bored nonchalance of a man who didn't especially care for his work.

I shuffled across the busy mezzanine and out to the taxi stands, not really having to act the part of a tired old man. I *was* beat. I had not been able to sleep on the flight over, nor had I even been able to rest my mind.

One recurring nasty thought kept drumming through my brain. If Hawk were indeed guilty—if he was in fact selling the NATO documents to the Russians—would he have told me? Or would he have played the part he had, involving me to the point that I would be killed as soon as AXE caught up with me?

That thought in itself was bad enough, but my beleaguered mind refused to leave it alone.

If Hawk was not guilty, on the other hand, whoever had set this up in the first place now had me in a position for a legal kill.

Yet what were Hawk's options if he was guilty? There was only one. He'd have to defect after the dust settled a bit. The first step in his defection would be my elimination. I was the only one at this moment who knew where he was.

With me gone, he'd have a clear shot at getting out. Probably through Canada.

I took a cab to a small *pensione* that I had stayed at once before many years ago, just off the Boulevard de la Gare, across the river from the Entrepot de Bercy, which is a huge warehouse district not too far from the Bois de Vincennes.

The concierge looked at me with a startled expression on his face. It was possible he vaguely recognized me, or thought he did, but he had the good grace to recover quickly as he took my passport and watched as I filled out the registration.

"Will *Monsieur* Sutherland be staying with us long?" he asked, and slid the card around so he could read it as he jotted down my room number.

"Three or four days, perhaps," I said, making my voice sound hoarse.

The man smiled broadly and handed me a key to a room on the fourth floor. "Our bellboy is temporarily indisposed, *monsieur*. If you would like to leave your bag here, I will have it sent up when he returns."

"It's not necessary," I said, returning his smile. Once I was out of sight, he would almost certainly open it to find out who I really was. "I'm stronger than I appear."

I picked up my suitcase, turned and went across the tiny lobby to the open elevator and went directly up to my room.

Before I laid down for some much needed rest, I reassembled my weapons, and using another of the photo booth pictures, made myself an international driver's license under the name Sutherland so that I could rent a car when it was time to leave for Brussels.

NATO headquarters would be like the Bastille as far as I was concerned, I figured. They would expect me to go there for the answers. Which I was going to do. But before I approached the place I needed a couple of wedges to break past their security. With any luck Sandry would provide one wedge for me with a name for the face she had drawn. I'd come up with the other.

It was nearly four in the afternoon by the time I arose, took a quick bath, dressed in my own, more comfortable clothes and presented myself at the desk.

The same concierge was there, with the same smile, when I stepped off the elevator and approached.

"Good afternoon *Monsieur* Sutherland," the man beamed. "I trust your room is satisfactory."

"Quite. I'm interested now in finding an English language rental library nearby."

"You are in luck. There are two very excellent libraries of that nature. What is it that you seek? A good novel perhaps?"

"I'm looking for recent newspapers."

"Then the library just off the Place d'Italie is your best," he said, and he gave me directions.

I thanked him and left the hotel, finding the library as

promised in a small glass-fronted building that housed several import shops as well.

A young, very good looking woman was seated at a small desk that looked out over the narrow street in the book lined front room. Toward the back, through a narrow door, I could see another book filled room, and up an iron spiral stairway, there were even more volumes on a balcony.

"*Monsieur*?" she looked up from her reading as I entered the shop.

I smiled at her. "I'm looking for some back issues of the World Herald Tribune," I said. "The Paris Edition."

"Yes?" the woman said. Her voice was soft, almost musical. "And how far back do you wish?"

"Just for the past week," I said.

She seemed almost disappointed, and I got the impression that if I had asked for something from a hundred years ago, something a little more difficult, she would have been much happier.

She got up from behind the desk and led me to the back room where today's editions of a dozen English language newspapers were spread out on racks as if they were laundry left out to dry. Below each rack there was a series of shelves each crammed with back issues of the newspaper above them.

"This goes back thirty days," the young woman explained. "If you wish earlier editions please ask. We keep them in the basement."

We were the only ones in the library, and I got the feeling that the young woman would love to get me alone in the basement.

"Thank you," I said.

"Do you require assistance?"

I shook my head, and she turned and went back to the

front of the shop where she sat down again at her desk.

Quickly I took out several issues of the World Herald Tribune for last week and spread them out on a small work table in the center of the cramped room, and began thumbing through the news pages, finding what I had come looking for within ten minutes.

On page seven of the newspaper for six days ago, was a brief article with the healine: SOVIET DIPLOMAT KILLED IN AUTO ACCIDENT.

There was no mention in the story of the documents that had been found on the man, of course, but they gave his name as Yuri Ivanovich Noskov, 43, attached to the Soviet Embassy in Brussels as a financial consultant.

He was in Paris for a short holiday, the newspaper reported, before returning for reassignment back home in Moscow.

For a moment I was drawing a blank. I had half expected that the courier would have been a member of the embassy's military liaison, or might even have been identified as KGB. Those would be the people most likely to be involved with such an operation.

But then it struck me that the dead man had been nothing more than a courier—at the most. At the least he had been a patsy. He had been given a package of documents to take back to Moscow. He had probably not even been told what they contained, just that they were very important and should be guarded with his life.

Somehow I was going to have to find out who Noskov had worked for. I was sure his position was well insulated from the top, but at least it was a start.

When I had replaced the newspapers on their shelf, I turned and went back to the front room of the library where the young woman looked up, the same hungry smile on her face.

"Did *monsieur* find what he was looking for?" she asked.

"I did, and thanks for your help," I said. "What is the fee?"

"For the newspapers there is no fee," she said. "If you would wish something else . . . perhaps something not on our shelves . . ." She let it trail off, but I knew exactly what she was suggesting.

"Perhaps another time," I said, making a mental note to change back into the old clothes to make myself look more down at the heels.

"Perhaps," she said, disappointed, and I left the shop.

Instead of returning directly to my hotel, I headed up one of the narrow side streets that led toward the river past the Gare d'Austerlitz, the trains rumbling into the ornate depot, and the traffic on the main intersection busy.

As I walked, I played out two scenarios in my mind. In the first Hawk was in Brussels, had signed for and received his document package, and then had gone directly back to his hotel. The package could have been switched there. But only if Hawk had been incredibly careless.

When he returned home, and no alarm was sounded about the fake signatures, the documents with his real signatures were passed on to the Soviets.

It just did not make sense. Why, if they had copies of the documents in the first place, did they take the risk of forging Hawk's signature before making the transfer?

In the second scenario, Hawk made copies of the documents and gave them to the Russians in Brussels.

Later he could claim that the documents in his safe were fakes.

Mandel had told me the lab boys had verified his signature. I had not seen them, so I had no direct knowledge.

Hawk, or Mandel or someone else?

No matter which way I looked at it though, no matter how hard I tried, the second scenario, the one in which Hawk was the traitor, seemed the most logical. Seemed the one with the least assumptions.

At any rate, the answers would lie in Brussels, I was sure.

If Sandry had been successful, and had managed to dig up a name and background for the sketch yesterday, it would be at *Madame* Rochard's tomorrow evening sometime.

I had one wedge for getting to the NATO traitor, but I needed the other. Who was the man? And more importantly who had hired him to assassinate me?

I stopped at a small café near the river, and had a light omelette with a couple of cognacs, before I went back to my hotel.

When I got back a new face was behind the desk, but the man was even more pleasant than the day concierge, and handed me my key with a huge smile.

The bit of fuzz I had placed between the door frame and the door itself was still in place, and the door knob was at exactly the same angle I had left it.

It would take AXE's operatives several days to catch up with me, I figured, although Brussels would be crawling with spotters, informants who knew me and legmen brought over to track me down.

Here in Paris I would be relatively safe for the time being, but in Brussels things would be considerably more difficult.

I lay down for awhile, but could not sleep, and after about an hour I got up, got dressed and left the hotel, aimlessly walking the back streets, sometimes near the river, sometimes blocks away from it.

For most of my life I have been a man with a relatively clear conscience. I've had the rare luck to be able to see what had to be done, and I've done it. No recriminations. No second thoughts. Just follow the clear path to the end of whatever assignment I've been on.

But this time everything seemed muddy and unclear to me. I felt like the traitor in this situation.

And then there was Hawk. No matter how many times I went over this case in my mind, he came out the guilty one. That conclusion was tearing me apart. If he was selling the Russians NATO documents I'd have to hear it from him. I didn't know how I would be able to handle it if I came up with the concrete proof that he indeed was the traitor.

Yet, despite everything else, there was a deep seated part of me that refused to believe Hawk could be guilty. I half suspected that if Hawk told me face to face that he was guilty, I still would have trouble accepting it.

The President believed Hawk was a traitor. Mandel and AXE believed he was a traitor. NATO knew Hawk was the traitor. Admiral Haiger and the CIA believed he was guilty.

All of them believed it. They all had convincing proof. And yet I had aligned myself against them all. Had aligned myself against my own country, for the sake of one old man who could offer me nothing more than his word.

The *coup de grâce* was Hawk's jumping.

I was at the river, just across from the magnificent Notre Dame, and I walked down the stone steps to the water's edge, where I found a bench and sat down.

I lit myself a cigarette, inhaling deeply, and shivered as I pulled up my coat collar against the damp chill of the night air.

It was just before midnight, and several pairs of lovers strolled arm in arm along the wide quay, lost in their own pleasures.

Hawk had jumped, but only—by his own admission—after he became convinced that Mandel had come up with at least a *prima facie* case against him.

He must have known that I would be the one assigned to come after him, so he had hired a hit man to meet me at the airport and take me out.

His fail safe against that not working was to wait at the cabin for me to show up, at which time he would convince me that he was right and everyone else was wrong.

He had read me perfectly. He knew that I would come to him alone. That I would cover my trail well. But he had been nervous just the same, and had asked me if I had hid my tracks.

I pulled at the cigarette, drawing the smoke deeply into my lungs.

His next step then would be to bail out. Across the border into Canada. Up to Nova Scotia, from there a private boat to Iceland perhaps. And finally Aeroflotz directly to Moscow for the hero's welcome.

If he was going to jump, he'd already be gone. He would not have remained at the cabin risking my success in unraveling his network.

"Christ," I said half under my breath. I had been the fool. He had played me like a virtuoso plays a Stradivarius, with finesse.

I flipped my cigarette away, stood up and, with

hands stuffed deeply into pockets, went back to my hotel.

There was nothing I could do this evening. But tomorrow I would get the answer the only way I knew how, no matter what it did to me.

The Paris dawn broke brilliantly clear, the smog blown away at least temporarily by a gentle but persistent southwest wind, and the air washed by a light rain that had fallen sometime in the early morning hours.

I dressed in one of the old suits and left the hotel around seven thirty, stopping a few blocks away at a sidewalk café where I dawdled over a breakfast of croissants and *café au lait*.

By nine I was at the main Telephone Exchange downtown, where I gave one of the counter clerks the number in the States I wanted to call, and paid for the first three minutes.

I was assigned a booth, and when I had the door closed I picked up the telephone just as it began ringing at the other end.

It was three in the morning on the East coast, but Hawk answered the phone on the second ring with his gruff hello and nothing more.

For several long seconds I sat holding the phone to my ear, the relief sweet, until Hawk's voice once again came over the international line.

"I expected your call Nick," he said.

"I—" I started to say.

"Don't worry about it," he said. "I expected it. I would have been disappointed in you had you not called."

"I'm sorry," was all I could manage.

"You should be," Hawk said, "but I understand.

You've got to understand now that you still have the same dilemma.''

"Sir?''

"I may have hung around here only long enough for you to make your verification call. Once you hang up I might skip. It would give me a few extra days.''

"I don't think so, sir. Not any more. And I'm sorry I ever doubted you.''

"Don't be a fool, Nick,'' Hawk snapped. "Doubt everything, including me. Everything!''

I quickly explained to Hawk what I had learned so far from the newspaper, and that I was waiting for Sandry's information to show up at *Madame* Rochard's. Once it came I was going directly to Brussels.

"Be careful,'' Hawk warned. "They'll be expecting you there.''

"I know,'' I said. "But if the answers are anywhere, they'll be at NATO headquarters.''

"Where are you staying in Paris?'' Hawk asked, and I told him the name of my hotel.

"I don't think they'll be looking for me here. They'll be setting up their watchdogs in Brussels.''

"You're probably right,'' Hawk said, and he sounded distracted. "Good luck.''

"Thank you sir,'' I said and hung up.

After I left the Telephone Exchange, I took a cab to the Hertz office just off the Champs Elysées where I rented a Fiat Spyder sportscar under the name Sutherland. Then I drove down past the Palais de Chaillot before I went across the river on the Boulevard de Grenelle and slowly past *Madame* Rochard's.

I had been using the bistro as a private, blind-letter drop for several years now, as had a number of other people, I was sure. In the eighteen hundreds the place had been a successful bordello, but after the first World

War, it had gradually changed character, finally becoming a chic nightclub—a place for assignations.

Even during the Nazi occupation of the city in World War II, *Madame* Rochard's was open for business as usual, and I had always figured the club would be in operation forever, ownership being handed down from one generation to the next in the Rochard family.

When I drove by this morning, however, it was closed. The wrought-iron tables and chairs that had always been set up in the front were gone, the front windows and door were boarded up, and a sign tacked to one of the posts holding up the ornate canvas awning informed passersby that the club had been permanently closed by order of the police.

As I passed the club I glanced up at the line of windows in the second floor and noticed a curtain moving, and then nothing. A moment later I was around the corner at the end of the block.

Madame Rochard's might have been closed for business, but the building was not deserted. I was sure there was someone upstairs.

I went back across town where I parked the Fiat a couple of blocks from my hotel, in a small attended parking lot along the river, and went the rest of the way on foot.

The day concierge was on duty, but instead of a smile on his face, he was scowling as I came up to the counter and asked for my key.

"We do not want any trouble *Monsieur* Sutherland," the normally affable man said.

Alarm bells began jangling along my nerves, but I forced my expression to remain calm. "Trouble?" I asked.

From the corner of my eye I could see two other people seated in the hotel lobby. One of them a very old man, and the other an old woman. Probably husband and wife. No danger.

"Trouble, *monsieur*," the concierge repeated. He leaned forward, a little closer to me and lowered his voice. "We would like it very much if you would terminate your visit with us."

"I don't understand."

"The police were here just a little while ago *monsieur*," the man explained. Every muscle in my body was tense. "They wanted to see your room. There was nothing I could do, you must understand."

"Are they here now?"

The concierge shook his head. "No, *monsieur*. They wanted to see your room, and nothing more. They said nothing else."

"I see," I said. I looked at my watch which showed it was just a little after ten. I had spoken to Hawk less than an hour ago, the thought flashed across my mind, but I shut it off. I was falling into the same trap as before.

The concierge had handed me my key, and I assured him there would be no trouble, but that I would nevertheless pack my bags and check out this morning so that everyone would feel more comfortable.

I took the elevator upstairs, and cautiously approached the door to my room. The piece of fuzz I used to mark the door was still in place, and the doorknob was still at the same cocked angle I had left it.

Something was drastically wrong here. Very wrong.

I turned and hurried back down the narrow corridor and took the elevator down to the desk where the concierge looked up at me with suspicion.

"Did the police enter my room?" I asked, keeping my voice low.

The concierge nodded. "I believe so."

I held out the key. "Then they must have jammed the lock somehow. My key doesn't work."

"It must work," the concierge said as he came around the counter and took it from me. "I will help you," he said.

The two of us went up in the elevator, and on the fourth floor the concierge went directly to my room where he placed the key in the lock. I didn't know what to expect, but I held back a few feet away from the door as the key turned easily in the lock.

The concierge was turning toward me, a smile on his face as he pushed open the door. But, before he could say anything a tremendous explosion blew the door and part of the wall out into the corridor in a blinding flash, half burying me in rubble, the ceiling threatening to collapse, and blood, bone and hunks of flesh flying everywhere.

FIVE

The wall had saved me from the major force of the blast that had been mostly directed toward the opening door; but the concierge had not been so lucky.

As I picked myself up from the smoldering rubble, my stomach flopped over several times. The man was no longer recognizably human. He had taken the brunt of the explosion straight on, and his body had been reduced to a mass of chopped meat and bone that was splattered up against the corridor walls at least fifty feet in both directions.

I was shook. It took me several seconds to get my bearings, and to realize that I could not hear a thing other than a dull ringing. Blood was streaming down from my nose, but other than that I had come out of it relatively unscathed.

I stumbled over the pile of debris and climbed into my room. The wall facing the street was half gone, but from the looks of things, I suspected the dynamite or plastique or whatever they had used, had been taped to the door so that the majority of the force had been directed outward toward the corridor.

I only had a couple of minutes before the authorities began showing up, so I had to hurry, although it was difficult at this moment to make my brain work properly.

My bed had been shoved up against one corner, but I managed somehow to push it up high enough so that I could pull my suitcase out from under it, with my all-important documents kit. Then I turned and went back out into the corridor.

It worried me that I couldn't hear anything; even more troublesome was the fact that the only person who knew I was staying at this hotel was David Hawk. The thought made me almost physically sick.

A number of people had come out of their rooms and were crowded in the corridor as I climbed over the pile of rubble and hurried toward the stairway.

A man wearing only a pair of trousers with no shirt, shoes or socks, stepped directly in my path, his mouth opening and closing. I stiff-armed him out of the way and he went down with a surprised, hurt look on his face, and two old women quickly got out of my way as I made the stairwell door.

By the time I reached the ground floor, the ringing in my ears was starting to fade and I could hear someone pounding on the stairs. It took me a moment to understand I was hearing my own footfalls.

The stairwell opened on a narrow vestibule—to the right it led back to the front lobby, to the left it led to a back door into the alley and straight ahead it led to the staff bathroom.

I could hear a great deal of commotion from the lobby and in the distance I was sure I heard the sound of sirens.

There was very little time left for me to get out of here, but I knew that if I left the hotel this way I would be picked up within a block, so I ducked into the bathroom.

My hair was a mess, blood had caked on my face from my nose and I was covered with plaster dust. My shoes were also coated with blood.

I went into the toilet stall where I opened my suitcase and quickly changed clothes as the sirens came closer, and from outside I could hear the fire engines and ambulances screeching to a halt.

When I had changed clothes, stuffing the others back into the suitcase, I washed off my face as best I could at the sink, combed my hair and then carefully opened the door to the vestibule.

There was even more commotion than before from the front of the building, and in the distance somewhere in the building I could hear a woman screaming, her voice high pitched and penetrating.

Quickly I slipped out of the bathroom, went across the vestibule and was outside and hurrying down the alleyway toward the street where a large crowd had gathered.

No one noticed me as I came from the alley and slipped along the fringes of the crowd. Within a couple of minutes I was well away from the hotel, my heart, which had been pounding nearly out of my chest, finally beginning to slow down.

Hawk was the only one who knew I was at the hotel. That thought kept running through my mind, and yet I felt as if I was missing something; missing some vital clue that would provide a satisfactory explanation.

I went around the block before cautiously approaching the parking lot where I had left the Fiat. As far as I could tell my car had not been staked out.

There was a great deal of traffic in and out of the lot, however, and the buildings across the street from it could have hidden an army of surveillance teams.

I went farther up the block where I stopped at a sidewalk café and ordered myself a cognac, as I continued to watch the activity in the lot.

The explosion had taken me completely by surprise—too completely by surprise—and I was sure now that I was missing something all important. Whoever was on my trail was just a step ahead of me. It was a very uncomfortable feeling.

If it had been Hawk, something I desperately did not want to believe, then he had worked very fast and efficiently. His team would have to have been already set up and waiting on the chance I would be coming to Paris. Once my hotel had been spotted, the bomb could have been easily set up within a few minutes.

I let a full half hour pass before I finally paid my check and went across the street to the parking lot where I approached a tan Mercedes two rows and a half a dozen cars up from mine.

My entry to the lot had elicited no unusual activity as far as I could see. No paneled vans were parked nearby. No one was loitering on the street. There was no glint of field glasses from the roof line. Nothing.

I took the car keys out of my pocket and went to my car where I opened the door on the passenger side. I stuffed my suitcase behind the front seat, then crawled over the gear shift where I quickly inspected the driver's side door. It had not been tampered with.

Before I put the key in the ignition, however, I got back out and opened the hood. There was nothing wrong there either; the car had not been booby-trapped. Whoever had set up the bomb in my hotel room had apparently figured it would do its job.

They knew about my hotel, but perhaps they didn't yet know about the car. I got back in behind the wheel, started the car and drove to the exit where I paid the attendant. Then I headed out of the city toward the north.

The day was bright and very warm, and despite the heavy traffic which required me to concentrate on my driving, I began to calm down and think this thing out logically.

As far as I could figure it there were three people who knew I was in Paris: Hawk, Sandry, and the concierge at my hotel, whom I was sure had recognized me.

This last possiblity, however, bothered me almost as much as the possibility that Hawk had sent someone after me.

If the concierge had indeed recognized me, and if for some reason he had told whoever had come looking for me that I was staying at his hotel, then he had been abused terribly.

It did not sound like an AXE operation, or even CIA. Our people tend not to involve innocent people that way.

I stopped at an inn for a late lunch just outside of Clermont which was a town of about seven thousand persons, thirty-five miles north of Paris.

The town was situated on the edge of the Paris industrial area that followed the Oise River to the east. Toward the northwest, however, was the beginning of wheat country, and the setting provided a peaceful backdrop for me to unwind before I had to go back into Paris.

Sitting at a table on the second floor balcony at the front of the inn, sipping a half bottle of Gamay Rothschild, I twice made the decision to find a telephone and call Hawk, telling him where I was. But both times I backed off almost immediately.

First, if Hawk *was* trying to have me killed, leading his people here would only involve the owners of this place in more trouble than they could handle. Second, if Hawk was *not* the one, my phoning him would accomplish absolutely nothing.

I also toyed with the idea of forgetting Paris and continuing on to Brussels, but that would be like jumping out of the frying pan directly into the fire. Besides, if Sandry had been successful and had sent the information to my blind-letter drop at *Madame* Rochard's, there was a possibility it would be there this evening.

And even if it was not there, I thought grimly, I was going to find out who was living upstairs, and why the place had been closed down.

After lunch I rented a room at the inn for just one night, took a long leisurely bath and then laid down for a couple of hours of rest.

By six I was up and dressed, and had made myself a new passport and international driver's license in the name of Mark Morgan.

I had a quick, light supper at the inn, and then drove into Clermont where I abandoned the Fiat a couple of blocks from the railroad station. There was a possibility that they had a description of the car, and driving it back into Paris would be asking for trouble.

The round-trip ticket was only twenty *francs* and put me in the city at the Gare du Nord at eight o'clock. But the last train back left Paris at eleven which gave me only three hours. It would be sufficient time unless I ran into some serious trouble.

It was a Friday night and the commuter train was packed to capacity with a noisy crowd of field workers going into the city for a night out. I kept to myself in one of the seats near the rear door, and when we finally pulled into the depot I was the first one off. After losing myself in the crowd, I went up to the street level and hailed a cab, directing the driver to take me to the Eiffel Tower.

It was nine o'clock and the Paris night life was just getting into full swing by the time I had paid the cabby and walked the last few blocks to *Madame* Rochard's.

As I turned the final corner a half a block up from the bistro, I was stopped in my tracks and hurriedly slipped back into the shadows.

The place was lit up and I could hear music coming from within. The wrought-iron tables and chairs had been replaced on the sidewalk, and were crammed with people. Even as I watched, white-coated waiters carrying trays ladened with food and drink scurried back and forth.

It was business as usual. Business as if nothing had ever happened, and yet this morning the place had been closed down by order of the police.

Madame Rochard's had been owned and operated since the early fifties by Jacques Rochard, a great-great-grandson of the original *Madame* Rochard. I had always picked up my messages from him personally. No one else was involved with the letter drop system.

Jacques was a ferret of a little man, with dark, shifty eyes, who ran a great establishment despite his philosophy that the only thing in life that really mattered was money.

Nothing was immoral, as far as Jacques was concerned, providing it paid well.

I was reasonably certain that he had been paid handsomely for closing his place earlier today, just as I was reasonably certain that the closing had something to do with my presence here in Paris.

There were two things that I wanted from Rochard, I thought, as I hurried around the block toward the back of the bistro. The first was my message from Sandry if it had come, and the second was the answer to why he had closed down this morning.

At the corner I found an old woman selling flowers from a pushcart and bought a dozen tea roses which she wrapped for me in newspaper.

Farther down the block, I went up the steps to an apartment building that was set back-to-back with Rochard's on the next street and rang the buzzer for one of the apartments on the second floor. The nameplate said it was occupied by *Madame* Martienne Villiers.

A woman's voice came over the speaker a moment later. *"Qui?"*

"I have flowers for a *Madame* Villiers," I said in French.

"Flowers?"

"Yes, flowers," I said.

"Moment," the woman replied and a second later the lock buzzed and I opened the door and went up the stairs.

By the time I reached the second floor Madame Villiers, who turned out to be a pleasant looking woman in her late forties or early fifties, was waiting for me. Her eyes lit up when she saw the package I was carrying.

I handed them to her with a smile.

"There is a card?" she said unwrapping the flowers.

"No, *madame*," I said. "I was just told to deliver this to your door and tell you they have come from a friend."

She handed me a one *franc* coin and went back into her apartment with a wide, radiant smile. Apparently she was convinced in her mind who her secret admirer was, and was pleased.

I had started down the stairs, but when her door was closed, I turned and silently hurried up to the top floor where I found the fire escape ladder to the roof.

There was no alleyway behind *Madame* Rochard's, and the roofs of all the buildings in the block were interconnected, forming a jagged, uneven umbrella.

It took me less than five minutes to work my way to the back of the apartment building and then over on to *Madame* Rochard's roof, where I lowered myself into a bathroom on the top floor through an iron-framed skylight.

Jacques's office and living quarters were on the second floor of the four-story building, but as soon as I let myself out into the dimly lit corridor I could hear the music and raucous laughter coming from below.

Silently I hurried down the stairs to the second floor where I eased open the door to a wide vestibule with two other doors, one of them solid which led to Rochard's apartment, and the other, a few steps away, frosted, which led to his office.

A light shone from the frosted-glass door, and as I stepped out into the vestibule I could hear someone talking from within.

I pulled out my Luger, levered a round into the firing chamber and clicked the safety off as I approached the door and put my ear to it.

The voices were those of men, but I could not recognize them, nor could I make out what they were saying, except that they sounded angry.

Carefully I eased the door latch down, raised the Luger, took a deep breath and shoved open the door, stepping quickly inside and to the left.

Jacques Rochard was seated behind his desk, a thin manila envelope in his right hand. Across from him was Bob Burns.

For an instant both men just stared at me, wide-eyed, but then recognition dawned on Rochard's face and he turned white. A split second later Burns knew me and he started to reach for his pistol.

"Don't," I snapped as I closed the door behind me.

"*Mon Dieu*," Rochard said half under his breath. "You are dead."

Burns's right hand was poised in midair just over the lapel of his coat. He had a strange look on his face. "Who was he?"

"The man at the hotel?" I asked. I remained standing, my back to the door.

Burns nodded.

"The concierge," I said. "But you should know that, Bob, your people set it up."

Burns shook his head. "We did not, Nick. And I know that one of them was the concierge. But I'm talking about the other body."

"There wasn't another body. Just the concierge."

"The police reports—" Burns started to say, but I cut him off.

"How did you know I was at the hotel?" I snapped impatiently.

"We didn't, Nick, I swear it. Not until after the explosion, although we figured you were here in Paris. We put a Class One watch on Sandry after your little game with her and when she mailed off the package to you care of this place, we came looking."

"Your people closed it down this morning?"

"They rented my club for the day," Rochard broke

in. "But I would not give them your letter." He held it out to me.

I moved away from the door and, keeping away from Burns, took the letter from the little man and stuffed it in my pocket.

"The papers this afternoon carried the story that an American tourist identified as Sutherland was killed in an explosion. The description they gave was close, and when State denied any such passport, we figured it had to be you. Of course the mess had already been cleared up by then, but we called everyone off. I was on my way back to Brussels; Mandel asked me to pick up Sandry's letter."

I reached in my breast pocket, took out my wallet and extracted two five-hundred *franc* notes, which I laid on Rochard's desk.

"We're leaving now Jacques. I want you to forget that we were ever here, do I make myself clear?" I said.

"Perfectly," Rochard said, his eyes gleaming as he scooped up the money. "But, *mon Dieu,* you gave me a fright when you came through that door. I thought I was seeing a ghost."

"I'll come back and kill you Jacques, if I find out that you've sold out to someone else," I said softly.

"Not to worry, *monsieur*," Rochard said.

"I have no worry," I said. "You should." I turned to Burns. "On your feet, Bob, we're getting out of here."

"I'm being taken hostage?" Burns asked, getting slowly to his feet.

"I just want to talk with you. When I'm finished you'll be free to leave."

Burns nodded.

"First your gun, though," I said, and Burns carefully pulled his .38 out of its holster and handed it to me. I pocketed it and reholstered my own weapon.

I let Burns go first, and when we were out in the vestibule I directed him toward the stairs which led down to the club.

"No one is downstairs waiting?" I asked.

"I told you, Nick, our people have been called off from this end. They're waiting for you to show up in Brussels, or at least they were."

"Your car outside?"

"Around the corner."

"How about your hotel room?"

"Already checked out," he said. "I was supposed to pick up the letter from Rochard and then head back to Brussels."

"What about Hawk?"

"We've got our people on it here in Europe, and back home Mandel has the entire service looking for him."

"But you?"

"I'm officially off the case."

I wanted to believe Burns, but something in the back of my mind kept telling me to be careful, everything wasn't as simple as it seemed.

Nevertheless, I was going to tell him everything I had learned, except of course where Hawk was hiding, and see what his reaction was. If he was telling me the truth, it was possible I could get him to help me. If he wasn't . . .

I let the thought trail off. If he wasn't telling the truth I'd have to deal with it somehow.

SIX

There was, as Burns had assured me, no one waiting for us in the club or outside on the street. We made it to his car, which was a Ford Cortina with Belgian tags, parked around the corner from the club, without incident, and Burns climbed in behind the wheel. I got in on the passenger side.

"Where are we going?" he asked, before he started the car.

"Brussels," I said. "We'll talk on the way."

He looked at me, an odd expression in his eyes. "Will you tell me something, Nick?" he asked in a soft voice.

I nodded.

"Have you had any contact with Hawk since you came to Paris?"

"Why do you ask?" I said, thinking uncomfortably about the Telephone Exchange. Hawk's number was recorded there because of my call.

Burns smiled wanly. "Let me put it another way. Did Hawk know you were staying at that hotel?"

"Yes he did," I said. "But I could have been spotted at the airport. And I'm sure the concierge recognized me."

Burns shook his head. "No one contacted us—"

"As far as you know," I interrupted.

"As far as I know," Burns corrected himself. "And I was the project leader over here." He looked out the windscreen toward *Madame* Rochard's. "That's number one. Number two is that AXE does not set innocent people up to be murdered. A bomb in a room is too crude for us. It's the sign of a desperate man."

Everything Burns was saying made sense—made too much sense—and I had already had the same thoughts. But hearing them now from someone else made me doubly uncomfortable.

"Your team was looking for me here in Paris, wasn't it?"

"Yes," Burns admitted. "We were taking the town apart, first the airports, train depots and even boat docks, and second your known haunts, as well as *Madame* Rochard's of course."

"Which is why you closed the club down."

Burns turned to me. "We figured if you came looking for Sandry's letter, and we were there, there'd be a fight. We didn't want anyone in the way."

"But you're saying to me that your people hadn't gotten to my hotel yet?"

"No we hadn't, Nick," Burns said with a straight face, and I believed him. It jibed with my own estimation that it would have taken a couple of days for AXE to run me down, even with an all out effort. Paris was a large city.

"And number three," Burns continued. "Assuming for just a moment that David Hawk is innocent, that he isn't a traitor, that he was somehow set up, who else could have gotten to your hotel?"

I didn't say a thing. I knew what was coming.

"Think it out, Nick," Burns said, his voice rising slightly. "AXE knew you were in Paris, but not where. Hawk, by your own admission not only knew you were in Paris, but knew your hotel. Did you have contact with anyone else?"

I shook my head.

"Then how in hell could someone else run you down faster than us? Who besides us and Hawk even knew you were coming to Paris, for Christ's sake?"

"Drive," I said.

"To Brussels tonight?" Burns asked.

"To Brussels . . . tonight," I repeated, and Burns started the car, flipped on the headlights and pulled away from the curb.

Across the river he turned right past the Palais de Chaillot, then headed north out beyond Le Bourget Airport, the night pleasantly warm.

Burns glanced over at me. "You're calling the shots, Nick. What do you want from me?"

"I've got nothing against you," I said. "As soon as we get to Brussels we're parting company."

"You amaze me," Burns said. "Right now everyone thinks you're dead. As soon as I get back I'll have to blow the whistle."

"But you don't think I'm working for whoever sold the documents."

"I think you're working with Hawk, but I think you

believe he's innocent," Burns corrected. "At least for the moment, though you're having difficulty with it."

"There's been no scuttlebutt to the contrary around the office?" I said clutching at straws.

"None," Burns said. "Hawk is missing on a field assignment. You've gone AWOL, and possibly defected."

"It still brings us back to my first question, Bob. Where does all this leave us?"

"It depends upon you. I think you'd better take a look at the letter Sandry sent you."

"You know what it contains?"

"We had a Class One on her," he said. "We know everything."

"Then why were you trying to get it back from Rochard?"

"We don't like information like that floating around," he said.

I pulled the envelope from my pocket and opened it with shaky hands. Inside were two pieces of paper, one of them the sketch Sandry had made for me. The other was what appeared to be a fairly detailed précis of a personnel dossier on a man identified as Aleksandr Petrovich Budakhin, 39, Leipzig, East Germany.

Budakhin, according to Sandry's notes, had attended school at Moscow State University, receiving a degree in political science. Sometime during the early sixties it was believed he had attended the KGB Higher School 101 outside of Moscow, and then in the early seventies he had been assigned as a Trade Mission specialist with the East German delegation to the United Nations.

He was a bachelor and lived alone at the UN diplomatic apartments in New York City, returning twice a year to East Germany for three weeks at a time.

The second half of the page was taken up with a detailed summary of his movements, especially while in New York, over the past ten years, followed at the bottom by the notation: REF INDEX 1A000AA.

I looked up. "What's the reference index and why wasn't Sandry able to get me the complete file?"

"The double A is a closed index," Burns said. "You should know that."

"Yes," I said. "But Sandry would have at least been able to find out the releasing authority. It would have added something. Was a conversion operation being run against—"

I suddenly stopped in mid-sentence, a sick feeling rising up from my gut. "Who is the releasing authority?" I asked.

"David Hawk," Burns said. He was looking at me out of the corner of his eyes.

"Do you know what the reference index contains?"

Burns nodded. "Yes I do. And I'm going to give it to you straight."

I didn't want to hear what I knew he was going to tell me. But I listened anyway, thinking of Hawk sitting at the end of the dilapidated dock.

"Six months ago Budakhin was converted. He was sending us some fairly low grade material, but he was Hawk's exclusive property. It was an arm's length operation. From what I can gather, Hawk supposedly had the idea Budakhin would eventually work his way higher into the government and sooner or later would become a class A source."

I looked down at the sketch Sandry had made for me. There was no mistaking his identity. He had been the man with the sword at the airport who had tried to kill me. He had been sent to assassinate me. He was Hawk's man. No one else's.

"How did you come up with Budakhin's description?" Burns asked.

"Shut up," I said tiredly, and Burns fell silent, concentrating on his driving as we sped through the night.

There it was again, I thought staring at the face in the sketch. No matter how hard I tried, no matter what I did, everything came back to Hawk. David Hawk, my mentor, my friend, the one man on this earth who I trusted implicitly. The only man I've never had the slightest doubt about. The only person I had never dreamed of questioning.

He had sat there at the end of the dock and told me straight-faced that he was not the traitor. He was not the traitor.

His voice echoed and re-echoed in my memory. And even now, after all that had happened, I found that I did not want to believe that Hawk was the traitor. Nor could I.

If not Hawk, then who, I asked myself. Or perhaps I was going at this all wrong.

I sat forward in the seat, pulled out a cigarette and lit it. Burns was watching me, glancing my way every now and then.

All the evidence so far pointed to Hawk as the traitor. *Pointed* to Hawk. Which did not necessarily mean he *was* actually the traitor. Just that the facts said he was.

For a moment even I had to balk at the tenuousness of the reasoning, but then I took it a step further.

The Soviets had every reason in the world to want Hawk out of the saddle. If they could accomplish it, the operation would provide them with two very real victories. The first would be Hawk's death. Eliminating him would remove a long standing thorn from the KGB's side. As an added benefit, Hawk's removal would effectively result in my own neutralization.

And the second was AXE itself. If Hawk was proved to be a traitor and was eliminated, it would take years for the service to recover. In fact it might never be the same again.

Budakhin would have been ticklish. The Soviets could have set him up for the false conversion, intending all along to send him after me, thus placing the blame squarely on Hawk's shoulders.

But how could the East Germans have approached Hawk without arousing the old man's suspicion?

That was question number one, for which I had no answer.

The NATO documents with his real signatures could have been switched, as Hawk suggested. But with my new line of reasoning it placed the documents in a different perspective.

Series 700 papers were the most important of all NATO secrets. There was no question of that. The Soviets would do anything to get their hands on them. And yet their courier in Paris, documents in hand, had been killed before he had made delivery.

For a moment I was drawing a blank. But for just a moment.

If they had had the documents in the first place—from a separate source within NATO; had them long enough to forge Hawk's signature—that meant two separate operations were being run here.

Number one was getting the Series 700s. Copies had been made. At least two sets. One to switch with Hawk; the other to be sent to the Soviet Union. The set with Hawk's real signature had been given to the courier, who was killed.

Number two, of course, was getting rid of Hawk and

possibly tumbling the entire service, which was why the courier had been killed.

Complicated. Ingenious. But full of holes, I thought, as I slumped back in my seat.

It still left my hotel in Paris. The only person who knew where I was staying was Hawk.

There was no way possible for the Russians to have checked the tens of thousands of hotel rooms in Paris and come up with my location so quickly—no matter how many legmen they had used. No way. In fact the Russians could not have known I was in Paris.

I had backed myself into another corner, but I didn't want to let it go.

Assume Hawk was not guilty. Assume the facts were engineered by the KGB.

How did they find me in Paris? A spotter at the airport? Why place a spotter there? Unless one of their bright boys took a chance that I'd be coming to Paris to check out the death of the courier.

That was the thinnest assumption of all, I unhappily admitted to myself. But for the moment it was the only way out of my corner—and still maintain Hawk's innocence.

There was one other puzzling aspect to this situation. It was something Burns had said to me at Rochard's.

We had driven a long ways in silence, passing through Noyon which was a small town sixty miles north of Paris, before I turned again to him.

"I've got one more question for you, Bob," I said, and he glanced at me.

"Go ahead," he said uncertainly.

"The two bodies in my hotel. Were you there? Did you actually see them?"

A startled expression crossed his features. "I was

just thinking about the same thing," he said. "No, we didn't get to the hotel until after the mess had been cleaned up."

"So how did you know there were two bodies?"

"The police report," Burns said. "And then I personally went to the morgue."

I sat forward at this. "You saw two bodies there?"

Burns nodded. "Neither one of them was recognizable. But the concierge was identified from his wallet, from his watch and from his dental work. The other body was clean. It could have been you though. Same general height and build."

My mind was racing, but I was fairly certain I had found a crack in the carefully prepared plot.

"There was no other man there, Bob," I said. "Just the concierge and myself." I quickly recounted for him everything I had done from the moment the concierge told me that the police had been there checking my room. When I had finished my story there was a deeply troubled look on Burns's face.

"Whether you believe anything I've told you, Bob, the presence of the third man in my room means something."

Burns waved me off with his right hand. "I know what you're going to say."

I waited for him to continue.

"If Hawk is the traitor, and if he was the only one who knew your hotel, and if he was the one who set up the bomb to take you out, who was the third man and why was he there?"

"I don't know who he was, for sure," I said. "But I think if he's ever identified we'll find out he was a Russian or an East German. That's less important than the fact that the third man proves that there were two separate groups who knew about my hotel. One setting up the bomb, and the second setting up a patsy for my protection.'' I fell silent for a moment. ''In the morning I want you to call the Paris police, officially, and ask them to perform an autopsy on the other man.''

''Looking for what?'' Burns asked.

''Bullet hole, knife wound, strangulation marks at the throat.''

''We may be out of luck,'' he said. ''From what I saw of the corpse, there wasn't much left from the chest up, and not much more below that.''

''Have them give it a try anyway,'' I insisted.

''I'll get on it first thing in the morning—'' he started to say, but then we looked at each other and smiled.

''Hawk is being framed,'' I said softly.

''I still don't know that for sure,'' he said. ''He is a bright old man. All this still could be his operation.''

''But?'' I prompted after a moment of silence.

''But I'm pretty well convinced that you're innocent, and that if and when Hawk *is* proven guilty, you'll take him out.''

I refolded Budakhin's sketch and Sandry's notes, stuffed them back into the envelope and handed it to Burns.

''You can turn this over in the morning. Tell them you picked it up at Rochard's.''

Burns took the envelope, with only a brief hesitation, and put it in his pocket.

I took his .38 from my pocket and handed it over as well.

He smiled. ''Aren't you taking a big chance, Nick?''

I shook my head. ''I don't think so. But since I'm officially dead I'll have a certain amount of freedom, providing I keep a relatively low profile. I've also got a legman now in NATO. Between the two of us we should be able to come up with the answers pretty quickly.''

Burns stuffed his pistol in his shoulder holster, sighed deeply and shrugged. ''Why do I get the feeling that I've gotten myself in over my head?''

''Because you have,'' I said lightly.

Burns glanced at me. ''If we're going to work together then, I'm going to have to know a lot more than I already do.''

''Agreed,'' I said, and quickly I told him everything that had happened to me from the moment I stepped off the plane at Washington National Airport and Budakhin tried to kill me, including my conversation later with Hawk, although I didn't tell Burns how or where I found the old man.

We continued through the night then in complete silence for at least ten minutes while Burns digested everything I had told him.

''There's a leak somewhere in NATO then,'' he said finally.

''Yes, but that's only part of it.''

''What do you want me to do?''

''I'll have to find a place to stay in Brussels, we'll have to set up a contact procedure, and you'll have to dig out a few answers for me.''

SEVEN

I had been to Brussels on several other occasions and it had always struck me as being one of the most beautiful cities in Europe. It is the largest city in Belgium, straddling the Senne River, and has tree-shaded boulevards running at every conceivable angle. There are dozens of lovely parks, wonderful old buildings and impressive monuments to dozens of heros and events.

During both wars Brussels had been occupied by the Germans, but today there was very little evidence of the strife the people had endured.

We had entered the city shortly after three in the morning, and Burns had driven me directly across town to the Holiday Inn just off the Brussels-Zaventem Autoroute on Koster Straat, a couple of miles southwest of the airport and less than four miles from NATO headquarters.

That had been two days ago and I was chafing at my

confinement, despite the agreement Burns and I had reached that we would wait a while for the dust to settle before we made our moves.

There was no mention made of me, of course, on either of the state television channels—one broadcasting in Flemish, the other in French—nor were there any articles concerning me in any of the newspapers I was able to get from the lobby.

I spent most of my time in my room on the second floor, overlooking the pool in the courtyard, having most of my meals sent up by room service.

The few times I did leave, once to the bar downstairs just for a couple of drinks and a change of scenery, convinced me that no alarm had been sounded over the Mark Morgan passport. No one paid me the slightest attention.

It was shortly before six in the evening of the second day when my telephone rang for the first time. I was sitting out on the balcony with a couple of bottles of Dutch beer, watching the swimmers in the pool, among them a couple of bikini-clad women who should have been dressed in sacks.

I hurried into the room, sliding the patio door closed, and picked up the phone on the third ring.

''Yes?'' I said cautiously.

''The tour bus is waiting for you, sir,'' Burns's voice came over the line. It was his signal that he was on a clear line.

''Very good,'' I replied. ''My headache is much better.''

''I'm calling from a phone booth downtown,'' Burns said, lowering his voice. ''Everything looks clear at my end. Officially you're dead, but that won't last long I'm afraid.''

"What happened?" I asked, something clutching at my gut.

"It was my fault," Burns admitted. "I had to give the Paris police a good reason before they'd perform a complete autopsy on the second man at your hotel. I told them we believed he may have been dead before the explosion occurred."

I groaned but said nothing.

"At any rate, they hit the jackpot. The man—still not identified—had been shot to death with an American military .45 automatic. The police are hopping mad. And now they want to know what the hell NATO has to do with it."

"It'll get back to Mandel," I said absently.

"Right," Burns said. "And he'll put two and two together and come asking me questions that I won't have any answers for."

I had to think this out. If Hawk had planted the other body in my hotel room to convince the opposition I had been killed in an explosion, who was the man? And why had Hawk ordered him killed in cold blood?

"No ID on the body?" I asked.

"None," Burns said, and he sounded distracted. "I think I've got a tail," he said a moment later.

"How about the other thing?" I asked quickly.

"I've got it and I'll come to you later tonight, but I'm going to have to cover my tracks."

"All right," I said. "But don't come to my room. Rent another one in a false name. Call me when you get here."

"Right," Burns said and he hung up.

I slowly replaced the phone on its cradle and went back out to the patio, where I settled down in my chair, took a sip of the beer and lit myself a cigarette.

I just could not imagine Hawk ordering an innocent man blown away like that and then planting his body in my room. It wasn't like him. And yet maybe the man hadn't been innocent. Maybe he had been a target all along. Still it seemed cold-blooded.

And secondly, why was Burns being tailed? Who didn't trust him? Or were the Russians watching him?

I felt so damned helpless sitting here, and yet without the information Burns would be bringing me tonight, I would be operating totally in the dark.

I took a shower about 7:30, then had room service send me up a couple of chicken sandwiches and a bottle of white wine. I was just finishing my meal when my phone rang again. It was Burns.

"We're in 308," he said.

"We?"

"I've definitely got a tail and I think it's one of ours. They followed me home from downtown and waited outside. I called my girlfriend and told her I was taking her to a motel."

"What does she know?" I snapped.

"Not a thing," Burns said lowering his voice. "She's in the shower right now." He hesitated a moment. "We're both married, Nick, so she's not going to say a thing. I've already explained to her that I've got to talk with someone for a few minutes before I get back to her."

"All right," I said. "Were you followed here?"

"Yes. They're downstairs, so whatever you do don't show your face anywhere."

My hand tightened on the telephone. "Are you coming right down?"

"Be there in two minutes," Burns said and he hung up.

This was starting to get uncomfortably tight, I thought as I set the phone down. Someone didn't trust Burns. But why? Was it because of his inquiries about the body in Paris?

I went to the patio doors, careful to keep out of sight, and closed the heavy drapes. Then I took out my Luger, levered a round into the chamber and flipped the safety off.

At the door I released the security chain, unlocked the dead bolt and stepped back.

A couple of minutes later someone knocked once, and I raised my gun. "Come on," I said.

The door swung open and Burns slipped inside, closing and locking it behind him. He was lugging a large suitcase.

I lowered my gun, clicking the safety on. "Anyone see you leave your room?"

"No," he said. He came across the room to the small table, shoved my dinner things aside and opened the suitcase.

Inside was a small, portable microfilm reader and a dozen or more spools of film. These he withdrew from the suitcase and laid them on the table.

"That's everything you asked for," he said. He was obviously nervous.

"Have you had a chance to look through any of it?" I asked.

"Just briefly. And frankly, Nick, I think you're grabbing at straws. I don't think you'll find anything in there. If you could tell me specifically what you want, then maybe I could . . ." He let it trail off.

"I don't know myself what I'm looking for," I

admitted. "But I've got to start somewhere."

"It's the start and the finish as far as I'm concerned," Burns said. "At least for a while. They could begin to get ugly."

"What do you mean?"

He looked closely at me. "I've got a wonderful wife and two kids, Nick," he started to say, but I cut him off.

"But you're fooling around with a married woman just the same and you're worried now that someone may pressure you into some answers using the situation as a lever."

"Exactly," he said, and my estimation of Burns went down several notches. He saw it from my expression. "I'm not making any excuses, Nick," he said defensively. "It's just the way it is. But it makes me vulnerable."

"Yeah," I said, troubled. Then I glanced down at the films. "Anything else I should know about?"

Burns followed my gaze. "No," he answered. "Everything you requested should be there."

"Don't worry about it then," I said looking up, although I was very worried. "Depending upon what I find, I'll probably be getting out of here, and out of your hair soon."

"Good," Burns said.

Again something clutched at my gut. The Burns I was seeing now was totally different from the Burns I had known before. Just two days ago in the car from Paris he had been willing, if not eager, to help. It made me uneasy.

After Burns left I packed my things so that if I had to leave quickly I could. Then I called down to the desk and ordered a rental car at my disposal immediately, and was assured one would be available at any time I'd care to stop at the desk and sign for it.

Then I set up the microfilm reader and inserted the first of the spools of film that Burns had brought me.

They were personnel and pay records for every man and woman on NATO's North Atlantic Council Defense Planning Committee, which consisted of fifteen principle subcommittees, each with a membership and staff of anywhere from a dozen to three dozen people.

It was going to be a long night, I figured, unless I got lucky. But I couldn't see how that was going to happen, because I didn't even know myself what I was looking for.

I was working nearly completely in the blind with only two factors for my search. The first was that whoever the traitor was, he or she had to have access to the Series 700 documents in the first place. The Defense Planning Committee not only handled those documents on a regular basis, it was the body that generated them.

The second factor was more speculation and hope than anything else. But I figured that if the traitor—or at least his or her contact—was a member of the Defense Planning Committee, he or she would have had to have made at least one mistake over the past eighteen months that this had been going one.

What that mistake might be, or even if it existed, was the thinnest of leads, but at the moment it was the only one.

Each of the subcommittees drew its leadership and staff from the fifteen member nations. Beginning at the Political subcommittee, I started wading through the personnel and pay records, which included brief dossiers of each person, his or her education, background and current circumstances, as well as month by month pay records, from whatever source, and dates and times of security checks and major projects handled.

The records, which were classified secret, were very complete, and as I worked through the night I began forming a picture of hundreds of highly dedicated men and women laboring for the common defense of their member nations. Their biggest battle, it seemed, was against the extremely complex bureaucracy that was made even more difficult by the varying political aims of each country.

Sometime in the early morning hours, I got up from my work, stretched and went into the bathroom where I took a quick, cold shower to clear my head.

NATO was a mess. Like the United Nations it had been conceived as a grand and noble organization, but unlike the UN it had sunk into a quagmire of petty bickering and political in-fighting. It was discouraging.

At eight in the morning I had room service send me up a couple of pots of coffee and a large breakfast of sausage, eggs and spinach, and then I slept for a few hours.

At noon I ate again and went back to work, but it wasn't until nearly nine that evening that I finally found what I was looking for, although I didn't recognize it at first.

I had worked my way through nearly every one of the subcommittees and was rapidly approaching the last group of dossiers on the second to the last roll, when something I had read earlier suddenly stuck out in my mind, and I hurried back to the spool of records for the Science Committee.

Specifically the dossier for a German. Bruno Dieter Heinzman. Slowly I read through his file trying to pick up what was bothering me.

The man had been born in Berlin in 1929, which made him fifty-two now. He had attended Gottingen University as a mathematics major from 1949—shortly after the university had been re-opened—to 1954, graduating with a masters degree.

He had then come to the United States where he had attended Harvard University as a political science major on a special cultural-exchange program, finally returning home to Bonn where he entered his government's service.

In 1972, he had been assigned to the German delegation to NATO where he had gradually worked his way up to the number two man on the Science Committee—more of an administrator over the scientists on the committee than anything else.

He returned home to Bonn several times a year at his government's expense. He was not, nor would he ever become a rich man on the money his government was providing him.

I stared at Heinzman's records trying to see exactly what it was that had bothered me the first time I had read through them.

And then it struck me. Suddenly and very hard. It was Heinzman's living arrangements here in Belgium. He had an apartment in Bonn, but here in Belgium he had a home thirty-five miles northwest of Brussels, as well as an apartment in town, near NATO headquarters.

For the next half hour I quickly looked through the dossiers on the seconds in command of the other fourteen subcommittees. Only two men other than Heinzman had their own homes here: one a Belgian national; the other an independently wealthy Canadian.

All the others—those in Heinzman's same circumstances—had apartments in town. Nothing else.

Several of them had apartments in questionably poor sections of town.

I sat back in my chair and lit myself a cigarette. Heinzman was not a wealthy man by any standard. Yet he could afford to maintain an apartment in town and a home in the country. How?

Somehow I had the feeling that I had found the mistake I had gone looking for. Only I was fairly certain that Heinzman was not the top man. If he was involved in this he was only the source, nothing more. But he was a start.

By ten o'clock I had showered, strapped on my weapons and dressed in dark trousers, a dark pullover and a navy blue blazer. I went down to the desk where I had them find me a cardboard box, which I brought back to my room and packed up the microfilm reader and spools.

I brought the box back to the desk and had them lock it in the hotel safe.

"A Mr. Bob Burns will be calling for this in the next day or so," I told the clerk, a pretty young woman, and she smiled and wrote down the information.

"Will there be anything else *Monsieur* Morgan?" she asked.

"I'll need a car for the next day or so," I said.

"*Oui*," she replied. "Something small, big?"

"Small," I said.

She checked a list and then brought me a form to sign. "A Triumph sedan is sufficient?" she asked as I signed for the car.

"Perfect," I said. And after I had shown her my international driver's license and paid the deposit, she had a boy bring the car around.

It was a small, plain gray, two-door coupe that looked nearly new. I tipped the young man, climbed in behind the wheel and drove around to the back of the motel where I parked in the shadows.

In the Triumph's glove compartment was a packet of courtesy maps which I took up to my room and spread out on the table, quickly finding the roads to the tiny town of Herselt near where Heinzman's country retreat was located.

I made a quick search of the room to make sure I was leaving nothing behind, then took my suitcase and hurried the back way down to the car.

The area around Heinzman's house was mostly heavily wooded with occasional farm fields hacked out of the forests. The roads were very narrow here, and in some cases cobblestoned. There was no traffic anywhere at this hour.

From the road, I could not see the house—and I had no idea how much property Heinzman had—or how far back the house was situated.

I drove another half mile down the road, after shutting out my headlights, and then parked as far over into the ditch as I could.

From my suitcase, I took out a small leather case that contained a number of tools—screwdrivers, pliers, wire cutters and a selection of lock picks—stuffed it into my jacket pocket and struck out through the woods on a diagonal path that hopefully would intersect with the driveway.

About fifty yards into the forest, and completely out of sight of the highway, was a tall wire mesh fence, on which was hung signs at hundred yard intervals in English, German, French and Flemish: WARNING HIGH VOLTAGE.

Heinzman liked his privacy, and yet he didn't want

that fact advertised to every passing motorist. This was
getting more and more interesting the farther I went.

Making as little noise as possible I worked my way
along the fence line, until I came to several trees growing close enough so that their branches overhung the
fence.

I climbed one of the trees, edged out on the branch,
which sagged under my weight dangerously close to the
top of the fence, and then jumped off, landing on all
fours like a cat.

For several long seconds I remained where I had
landed, holding my breath, straining my senses to pick
up a sound, any sound. But there was nothing. The
night air was nearly perfectly still except for the occasional sighing of the wind in the upper branches of the
trees.

There was no moon, for which I was grateful, but the
lack of light made the going difficult. The land rose up
toward a low hump, and when I got to the top I could
see down toward the driveway about a hundred yards
away. But farther into the property I was able to pick
out the faint glow of lights and I headed that way,
parallel to the driveway.

Fifteen minutes later I was standing in the deep
shadows of the forest at the edge of a wide, well-tended
lawn and flower garden fronting a huge three story
mansion that had to contain at least two or three dozen
rooms. I don't know what I had expected to find, but it
certainly wasn't anything this grand.

A huge granite porch, with balustrades and statuary,
ran nearly the entire length of the house, centering on a
large, ornately carved wooden door. Colored lights
illuminated the front of the house that bristled with
balconies, a dozen or more chimneys and windows
each with its own awning.

The grounds surrounding the house were well lit as well, almost as if Heinzman had expected company this night.

No lights shone from within the house, however, but that was not unexpected; it was well after one in the morning.

Keeping out of sight, I made a wide circle through the woods until I was in position at the rear of the house where there was a large garage and several other smaller buildings.

None of this was making any sense. The house and grounds had to be worth at least several million dollars. Spies, especially those at Heinzman's level, just did not make that kind of money. Those who did never spent it this ostentatiously.

I stepped out of the protection of the woods, feeling suddenly very exposed, and raced across an open space to the rear of the garage, and then worked my way to the corner of the building where I paused for just a moment.

The rear of the house was not as well lit as the front had been, but the windows here, which flanked another wide porch onto which a set of French doors opened, were also dark.

I took my Luger out, snapped the safety off and, keeping low edged around the corner of the garage, raced across the fifty yards of pavement to the house, noiselessly mounting the steps to the French doors where I flattened myself against the wall.

No alarm was sounded, and after a few seconds my breathing slowed down and I carefully peered through the windowpanes in the door.

I was looking down a wide corridor, doors on either side of it, that opened near the front of the house onto what appeared to be a wide entry hall, with a formal staircase. I could see the inside of the main front door, but the only illumination in the house came from the outside lights shining in the windows.

Shifting the Luger to my left hand I tried the door handle, which turned easily, and the door silently swung open on its hinges.

For just an instant some inner warning system made me hesitate. There was something drastically wrong. I could feel it thick in the night air. There was extreme danger here. But there was also the possibility of finding some of the answers I was looking for.

I stepped into the corridor, softly closing the door behind me, and went immediately to the front entry hall where I stopped a moment beside the wide staircase that curved up to a second-floor balcony.

The house was silent except for what sounded like the ticking of a large clock somewhere to my right.

Two other corridors led from the entry hall; one into what appeared to be a large, formal dining room, and the other, to my right, led into a conservatory. I could see the edge of a concert grand piano through the opening.

To the left of that corridor was a set of wide double doors, one of them half open. From the dim light I could just make out a large desk and what appeared to be floor to ceiling book cases. Heinzman's study.

I edged away from the staircase and looked up toward the balcony, half expecting to see someone standing there, but there was no one.

Quickly I crossed the entry hall, moving silently on the balls of my feet, and slipped into the study, closing the door behind me.

The room was large and furnished with the desk, a couple of chairs and a long leather couch in front of which stood a heavy coffee table.

The walls were mostly book-lined, with a scattering of well-framed paintings here and there and a sideboard bar in one corner.

I went immediately to the desk, where I sat down, holstered my gun, pulled out my tool kit and selected a lock pick. In a few seconds I had the drawer lock picked and I was going through the contents of the desk.

Almost immediately I found a leather-bound notebook with the German word *VERABREDUNGS* stamped in gold on the cover. Heinzman's appointment's book.

I started to thumb through it when I came across a scrap of paper on which was written the same signature at least a dozen times. For a long moment I stared at the slip, conscious of nothing other than my own heartbeat.

Someone, presumably Heinzman himself, had practiced writing David Hawk's signature over and over again. And the forgeries were good. Very good.

I stuffed the scrap of paper back where I had found it and slipped the book into my coat pocket. There would be time later to look through Heinzman's appointments.

I had found one clue—inconclusive, but it was a start. Now if I could find NATO documents with Hawk's signature.

As I was bending down to open the bottom drawer of the desk I was aware of a movement at the door, but before I could straighten up, the lights had come on.

EIGHT

The largest man I have ever seen in my life stood, framed in the doorway, pointing a .45 automatic at me, an idiotic grin on his huge, bearded face. He had to be at least seven feet tall and must have weighed in excess of three hundred pounds. The gun looked like a tiny toy in his massive paw.

I ducked down behind the desk at the same moment he fired, the shot going high, breaking a window behind me and sounding like a cannon going off in a drain pipe.

Shoving the desk chair away from me with my left foot I pulled out my Luger and flipped the safety off.

For a long moment there was silence, but then the big man laughed, the sound ominous. I could hear him coming across the room toward me and my grip tightened on the trigger.

The desk, which was nearly the size of a football field and had to weigh in the neighborhood of seven or eight hundred pounds, was suddenly flung aside with a tremendous crash. I swiveled around as the big man reached for me, and I managed to fire two shots at point-blank range before he batted Wilhelmina out of my hand with a huge paw.

In the next instant he had grabbed the front of my jacket and yanked me to my feet, tossing me half way across the room against one of the bookcases, as if I was nothing more than a rag doll.

There were two large, dark stains spreading across his right shoulder where I had shot him, but he didn't seem to be the least bit affected by his wounds as he lumbered across the room.

I managed to scramble to my feet and duck under his next blow as I slipped my stiletto from its chamois case under my right coat sleeve.

The big man spun around and started for me, but then hesitated a moment when he saw the gleam of the long, razor-sharp blade that I was shifting from hand to hand.

Under the best of circumstances I figured I had very little hope of beating this monster in a fair fight. And now my Luger lay on the floor across the room and my back felt almost as if it had been broken from where I had been thrown against the bookcase.

The only advantage I had over him was my speed, but all it would take to put me permanently out of commission would be one solid blow from either of his massive fists.

I edged to the left, toward the door, but he laughed, the noise coming from deep within his chest.

''There is no escape,'' he said in guttural German.

He was about ten feet away from me, his back toward the door to the entry hall. To my right was the over-turned desk, and I suddenly realized what I was going to have to do if I was going to have any chance at all of surviving.

I feinted to the left, but he followed my move, edging a little closer to me.

Then I laughed. I was going to have to make him mad. Make him act out of blind rage. "Tell me something you Nazi pig," I said.

The big man stiffened, color coming almost immediately to his face.

"Who was your mother?" I asked in street German. "The whore of Berlin? Is that so?"

Now he bellowed with rage and lunged toward me. At that moment I swung out with the stiletto, opening a large gash on his right arm, and then leaped to the right, jumping around the over-turned desk.

The big man bellowed again as he swiveled on his left heel and charged, stumbling almost immediately over the desk. As he was falling toward me, I stepped aside, and grasping the stiletto in both hands buried it to the hilt in his back just below his right shoulder.

The man screamed in pain as he struggled back to his feet like an enraged bull. In that moment, however, I was back around the desk and across the room where I scooped up Wilhelmina.

Any ordinary man would have been long dead, or at least out of commission by now with two bullet wounds in his shoulder, a knife gash in his arm and a nine-inch stiletto buried in his back, but that damage had done nothing more to him than make him insanely mad.

He charged me, both hands outstretched, as I stepped back against the wall and emptied my Luger into his chest.

The first three shots seemed to have no effect, but the next two slowed him down. As I continued to pull the trigger, the noise deafening in the confines of the room, he stepped back finally and sagged down to one knee, blood coming to his mouth and nose.

"No escape . . ." he coughed, but he would not go down. Instead he grappled at his back for the stiletto buried there.

A siren suddenly started to wail in the corridor, and I could hear the sounds of several men shouting and running across the entry hall.

Quickly I took a fresh clip of ammunition from my pocket and reloaded my gun as I rushed across the room to the desk chair. Stuffing the Luger in my pocket for a moment, I picked up the chair and threw it through the window which shattered in a million pieces.

I was about to jump out onto the long, ground-floor balcony when something hot and very sharp slammed into my left shoulder, causing me to stumble and almost fall.

Instantly my vision began to blur and I could feel the bile rise up in my stomach, and I turned around.

The big man had pulled my stiletto out of his back, had stood up and had thrown it at me, burying it a couple of inches in my shoulder. He was staggering toward me as I raised my Luger and fired point blank into his face which erupted in a gruesome mass of blood and bone, and he finally went down like a felled tree.

The study door was swinging open as I managed to turn, climb up on the windowsill and jump down to the balcony.

To the left four men in some kind of military uniforms were just coming around the house, so I turned to the right, hurried along the balcony and then jumped over the rail to the soft ground about eight feet below.

When I landed the shock sent waves of pain coursing through my body from the knife wound in my back, almost causing me to pass out. But somehow I was running across the lawn, keeping low and dodging from left to right toward the woods less than fifty yards away.

In the distance, toward the driveway, I could hear a truck starting up, and behind me someone shouted "Halt," in German, but I kept running.

Ten yards away from the woods they opened fire at me with automatic weapons, some of the bullets snapping into the soft ground around me, while others went high, whining off the trees and branches ahead of me.

Then I was stumbling into the brush, and within a few seconds I was out of sight of the house, although I could still hear the commotion of a great many men behind me.

A couple of hundred yards farther into the comparative safety of the forest, I stopped and leaned against a tree, my breath coming in ragged gasps and the pain at my shoulder making my head throb.

Somehow I managed to reach back and grasp the handle of the stiletto. I gritted my teeth, took a deep breath and pulled the blade out of my shoulder, my stomach churning and my vision seriously blurring.

I laid the bloody knife on the ground and took off my coat, struggled out my shoulder holster harness and then took of my shirt, which I folded into a thick pad.

My fingers felt like fat sausages as I reached back and held the folded shirt against the wound in my shoulder and managed to get my shoulder holster harness back on, strapping it as tight as it would go to hold the makeshift bandage in place.

When I had my coat back on, I wiped the stiletto off on some fallen leaves and slipped it back in its case. Then, Luger in hand, I headed through the woods making a wide circle again toward the rear of the house.

There was no doubt in my mind that they had found my car by now, parked along the side of the highway, and had either taken it away or had staked it out against the possiblity I would try for it.

The last place they would expect me to head for, I figured would be back to the house. If Heinzman himself was there, I could use him as a hostage for my escape.

I suppose I would have actually tried it, except that I stumbled across the creek at the same time I heard the dogs barking from somewhere behind me.

Somehow I had gotten turned around in the dark and had headed not only away from the highway, but away from the house as well.

For a long moment I stood at the edge of the stream, which was less than ten yards wide and nearly covered with overhanging branches from the thickly growing trees, as I tried to gauge the distance and direction of the dogs. But sounds were confusing in the forest, and after a few moments I wasn't sure if they were behind me or ahead of me.

Even if I could find the house now, I knew it would be useless. The dogs would just follow me and I would be trapped.

Heinzman was the key to this entire affair, and his appointments book with the scrap of paper inside was the first solid proof I had so far that Hawk had indeed been framed. I had to get away with it.

I stepped down off the bank into the water, which was ice cold, nearly falling when I stumbled over some slippery rocks, listened again for the dogs, which seemed much closer now, and then headed down stream, the water just over my waist.

The creek was moving much faster than I expected it would, and after less than a hundred yards, I knew that I would not be able to keep this up very long.

The water was so cold I had lost most of the feeling in my legs and it was nearly impossible to keep on my feet. At times the baying dogs seemed very close, while at other times they seemed very far from me.

For a while I struggled along near the riverbank, pulling myself forward with low lying branches, but it soon became too difficult because of fallen logs and jumbles of rocks.

For a time I tried to swim with the current, but that too was nearly impossible because of the weight of my clothes and weapons, as well as the wound in my left shoulder which made that arm almost useless.

At some point later in the early morning hours I found myself standing in chest-deep water, holding onto the gunwhales of a small, flat wooden boat tied to a fallen log.

My heart was racing and I could hear the blood pounding in my ears, mixed with the soothing sounds of water burbling.

I cocked my head to listen for the sounds of the baying dogs, but I couldn't hear them any longer. They were either gone or they were too far behind now.

The creek was much wider here and the current seemed even stronger. I tried to make my brain work, to envision the map of this area I had studied back at my hotel room, but everything seemed fuzzy and out of focus.

Painfully I heaved myself out of the water and into the bottom of the boat where I lay panting for several long seconds. Finally, gathering up what little strength I had left, I withdrew my stiletto and reached up to the bow where I sawed through the thick rope. When it finally parted, the little boat swung around backwards, bumping against a rock, and then slid out into the middle of the stream, gathering speed as the current caught it, and I drifted in and out of consciousness.

Sometime around dawn I came half awake, certain I was hearing the sounds of a helicopter, but then that faded and I fell asleep again.

Later I awoke to the sounds of gunfire in the distance, but again I wasn't sure if I was hallucinating or I was actually hearing what I thought I was.

It was raining, I began to realize, and I was shivering violently, the motion causing the pain to come at me in waves.

I tried to sit up in the boat, but a blinding flash of intense heat tore into my back, causing me to cry out, and then everything seemed to go fuzzy and soft, and finally there was nothing.

The sun was streaming through the large windows when I gradually came out of dreamless sleep, and for a long time I was content to be laying nude on my stomach, warm and free from pain. I was in a four-poster bed, and across the room near the windows was a pair of chintz-covered easy chairs, and to the left against the wall was a large, ornately carved wooden wardrobe. To the right against the opposite wall was a low, frilly table loaded with perfume and make-up bottles, behind which was a large mirror.

I was in a woman's room, obviously, but how I had gotten here was puzzling for the moment. Then it struck me: Heinzman, the fight with the big man, the forest, the stream, the boat. I shoved the covers back and got out of bed, the sudden movement making me weak and dizzy.

My shoulder had been expertly bandaged and, although it was stiff, there was very little pain.

When I regained my equilibrium, I shuffled across the room to the windows and looked outside. The room was on the second floor of what appeared to be a huge house, at least as large as Heinzman's mansion. Across a wide front lawn was a patch of forest that sloped sharply downward to a wide river along which a string of coal barges was being pulled by a tug.

"It's the Demer River," a soft, feminine voice said from behind me. "And you have a lovely derrière."

I spun around as a tall, strikingly beautiful woman of about thirty-five closed the door and leaned back against it. She had long dark hair, large dark eyes and high, delicate cheekbones. She was dressed in riding clothes, her tall boots highly polished and an ornate gold crest at the breast pocket of her red jacket.

She smiled. "Your front is even better," she said. "Although from the looks of you I'd have to say you've been in a number of nasty fights in the past."

"Who are you?" I said, not moving from the window. My voice was hoarse.

"Formally, I'm the Countess Maria Elizabeth Anne Giscard-d'Amberville," she said smiling. "My friends call me Anne. And how about you *Monsieur* Morgan—are you a criminal or a policeman?"

"Neither," I said, "but policeman is closest."

She pouted. "How boring. I'd hoped you would turn out to be a mysterious cat burglar, or perhaps a professional assassin."

"How did I come to be here—" I started to ask, but she pushed away from the door and waved off my question.

"There are clothes that should fit you in the closet, along with your things, including your nasty weapons and *Monsieur* Heinzman's appointments book." She looked at her watch. "It is nearly noon and I imagine you are famished. As soon as you're dressed you may join me for lunch on the back patio.'' She gazed appreciatively at me for a long moment and then turned and left the room.

The wardrobe was filled with a man's clothes that fit me reasonably well, and when I was dressed in tan slacks, a light pullover sweater and soft dress boots, I found my weapons on a shelf and strapped them on, donning a cream-colored brown blazer with the same gold crest at its pocket as adorned the woman's riding jacket.

Henizman's appointments book was also on the shelf along with my wallet, passport and other papers. These I stuffed in my pockets and then left the room, finding my way downstairs and to the rear of the house where the countess was waiting for me outside on a large stone patio overlooking a vast flower garden.

She was seated at a glass-topped wrought-iron table around which were four chairs. To her left was a matching serving cart on which were covered silver serving dishes and a silver coffee pot.

''Your shoulder feels better?'' she asked pleasantly as I came across the patio to her and sat down.

''It's a little stiff, other than that it's fine,'' I said as she poured me a cup of coffee and handed it across the table. ''Who was the doctor?''

''A friend from Brussels,'' she said. ''A very discreet friend. You will have no worry from him.''

I took a sip of the coffee. ''How long have I been here?''

''This is the fifth day,'' the woman said and I nearly dropped my cup. ''Henri insisted you be hospitalized, but I would not allow it.''

Five days. It seemed impossible. ''Does anyone else know I'm here?''

The woman shook her head. "No one outside my household staff, and Henri, the doctor. Are you dangerous?"

"You have a husband?" I asked.

She laughed out loud. "My husband has two passions," she said. "One are his flowers, which he supposes pacifies me. And the other is his gambling which is nothing more than the means for him to chase the skirts. He has been at the casino in Spa all week. After next week he'll probably be going on to Baden-Baden or perhaps even Monaco if the weather turns chilly."

I was going to have to get out of here, and very soon. There was no telling what had broken loose over the past five days.

"Before you leave," she said as if she had read my mind, "you must first have something to eat, and then tell me why you have stolen *Monsier* Heinzman's appointments book. Is it because he meets with the Russians? Is he a spy?"

"Russians?" I said. The woman was amazing.

She looked sharply at me for a moment. "Of course," she said half to herself. "You had no chance to read his journal. You were wounded in your escape."

I waited for her to continue.

"My gardener found you half dead in the bottom of the little boat near our dock," she said. "He brought you up to the house, where we went through your things once we had called the doctor. I read *Monsieur* Heinzman's appointments book. He meets regularly, at least once a month, with a man named Anatoli Oleg Grechko at the Skaldia-Volga assembly plant near Brussels."

"You know Heinzman?" I asked.

She nodded, a sour expression coming to her face. "I

have no love for *Monsieur* Henizman, nor any love for the Russians." She sat forward. "But don't you find it delicious that a NATO officer meets regularly with a Russian?"

"Very," I said, for want of anything better to say.

"Indeed," she said, and she sat back. "Then if you're not a criminal, it must mean you are a spy catcher. In which case I will help you."

NINE

The Countess and I sat at opposite sides of her desk, staring at each other as she slowly replaced the telephone on its cradle. Her complexion had turned white and her lower lip quivered.

"His wife was quite hysterical," she said, her voice husky.

I felt sorry for her, but despite my protests earlier in the afternoon, she had threatened to call the police unless I allowed her to help me. It was all a big game to her. Only now the game had turned ugly.

"Then it's true, Burns is dead," I said.

She nodded. "Did Heinzman have him killed?"

I had told her only bits and pieces of the story, and now I shook my head, leaned forward and reached across the desk for her hand. "It's more complicated than that Anne," I said gently. "Bob Burns was a policeman like me, and together we were working on this case.''

"But you are working here in Belgium, illegally," she said.

"Technically, yes," I admitted.

"This case . . . it involves Heinzman?"

"Yes it involves Heinzman," I said nodding. ''But it also involves other, even more desperate men.''

"Such as the Russian Grechko, at the auto factory?"

Again I nodded. Her telephone call for Burns first at NATO headquarters in Brussels and then just moments ago to his home, had no doubt been recorded. Under normal circumstances it would have meant nothing. She was just another female after him. But now questions would be asked about her connection with him. And very quickly someone was going to put the facts together and come looking for me here. I was going to have to get away, and yet I didn't want to leave the Countess to her own defense. If they felt she had been involved with me, they would kill her just like they had killed Burns.

No doubt Heinzman's people had traced down my rental car back to the Holiday Inn—the same Holiday Inn where Burns had registered with his mistress. Combined with his inquiries with the Paris police about the identity of the second man in my hotel room, they had come to the conclusion that Burns had been helping me.

They had killed him for it.

Heinzman's estate was less than twenty miles from here, and I was missing. Those facts combined with the call from the Countess, would be like a bright neon sign.

I stood up, came around the desk and helped her to

her feet and led her out of the drawing room where she had made the phone calls.

"I want you to pack a few things, and then you're getting out of here."

She looked at me. "Where will I go?"

"To your husband at Spa," I said, but she shook her head.

"Never," she insisted. "Heinzman is involved with this and I'm going to help you."

I shook my head. "What have you got against Heinzman?"

She flared. "He is a pig!"

"What did he do to you?" I asked, taking her shoulders in my hands and turning her around so that we were facing each other.

"I was riding one day and strayed onto his property. He had me brought to his house, where a brute of a man beat me with a walking stick. I told my husband but he just laughed. Said I deserved the spanking."

I couldn't believe what I was hearing. "People don't act that way," I said. "Just for straying on his land? It's insane."

"I used to ride there all the time. He telephoned me a few times and told me to stay away from him, but I just laughed. I have ridden those lands since I was a child."

Suddenly I understood the Countess Giscard-d'Amberville. She had always been a child. Spoiled. Petulent. Bored. But with a dangerous misconception of what the world and real people were all about. It explained her odd behavior over my presence.

I was definitely going to have to get her out of the way, and quickly.

"Have you got an automobile I can use?" I asked.

"Yes. There are several out in the garage. Take your pick."

"Fine," I said. "I've decided that you can help, afterall. Between us we should be able to stop Heinzman."

Her face lit up. "Good," she said. "Will you kill him tonight?"

I nodded. "Probably, but the other men I told you about—the ones who are running this operation—are all in Zurich."

"Zurich?" she said confused.

"Yes. I'll take you to the airport where you can catch a plane for Zurich this afternoon. I want you to check into a hotel there and wait for me. I shouldn't be more than a few days at the most."

"I want to stay with you—" she started, but I cut her off.

"You said you wanted to help," I told her sternly. "Well, I need a decoy. By now they probably know I'm here. If you run off to Zurich—to their headquarters—they'll expect that I'll not be far behind. You'll be able to draw them out into the open. Do you understand?"

"Yes," she said. "But will it be dangerous?" I almost laughed with pity.

"Very," I said, keeping a straight face. "But we must hurry. They're probably on their way here now."

"Good," she said with delight, as she turned and started up the stairs to her room.

"I'll bring a car around," I called after her.

"Be just a second," she called back over her shoulder.

I hurried through the house and out the back door where I ran into the gardener who had fished me out of the river. He was an old man, dressed in rough clothing with a cloth cap set at a jaunty angle on his head.

"Countess d'Amberville and I are leaving for Paris

within the next few minutes," I told him.

He nodded. "Very good sir." His expression was stern, almost disapproving.

"You may inform the rest of the staff. She won't be back for at least a week."

"Yes sir," the man said, a flicker of a smile playing at the corner of his mouth.

I hurried across a wide driveway and entered the huge garage which had spaces for a half a dozen cars. There were four parked inside including a Rolls, a large Mercedes limousine, a perfectly preserved MG-TD sportscar and an Alfa Romeo Spyder coupe.

The Alfa would be the least conspicuous, I figured, so I drove it out of the garage and around to the front of the house.

Inside I went upstairs where the Countess was just closing two suitcases that she had hastily packed. Earlier this afternoon she had changed out of her riding clothes, and she looked ready to go now.

"Money?" I asked, and she nodded. "Passport?" She nodded again.

"You will come to me in Zurich?" she asked.

"Yes," I lied to her. "But you must wait for me. I may be as long as a week."

"I'll wait," she said, and I grabbed her two suitcases and we headed downstairs to the car.

"I told your staff that we were going to Paris together," I said as we got outside.

She laughed. "Delicious. It'll get back to my husband. God only knows what he'll do. Probably come to Paris looking for us."

The Countess chattered like a little girl going on a holiday all the way into Brussels' Zaventem Airport, where I booked her on the next flight to Zurich which left in two-and-a-half hours.

I was taking a risk coming into Brussels in the daylight, but I didn't think they'd expect me to show up back here. At least not so soon.

After I had her bags checked, I waited with her in a dark corner of one of the airport bars, where she talked almost nonstop about her boring life, her boring husband, her boring house, and of Heinzman, who deserved everything he was going to get.

When they finally called her flight she kissed me passionately goodbye as if we had been lovers for a long time, and then she was gone . . . to safety I sincerely hoped.

It was nearly seven o'clock by the time I got away from the airport terminal and retrieved the Alfa from the car park.

Earlier this afternoon when I had read through Heinzman's appointments book I had known exactly what I was going to have to do this evening.

The Countess had been correct when she had told me that Heinzman had been meeting with a man named Grechko who worked at the Skaldia-Volga automobile plant here in Brussels.

The meetings had been going on at irregular intervals over the past eighteen months, never at the plant itself, but always somewhere within the city proper, usually at a restaurant, library or museum.

The Countess had known that the auto plant was a Soviet operation where *Moskvich* sedans were assembled for sale in Europe. But what she had not known was that the S-V plant was little more than a front for Soviet KGB operations.

The plant was located near the airport and less than two miles from NATO headquarters itself. And, unlike any other auto assembly plant in the world, the Skaldia-Volga factory buildings fairly bristled with communications antennas and microwave dishes.

The Belgians tolerated the Soviet presence only because the new, ultra-modern factory provided jobs for more than a thousand locals. And except for the electronic eavesdropping on NATO headquarters, the Russians at the plant had always kept very low key, careful to avoid any kind of an incident.

In fact one of Burns's jobs as AXE liaison to NATO had been to keep watch on the factory in case the Russians had ever decided to mount an operation of some kind.

Either the Russians had been too slick or Burns had made one too many mistakes, because he had apparently never tumbled to the fact that Heinzman had been meeting with an S-V representative.

Traffic was fairly light at this hour as I headed away from the airport on the Steenweg Highway and almost immediately I could see the auto plant across a wide, grassy field as a vast conglomerate of low, gray buildings. The administrative center, however, was a four-story edifice of glass and steel at the end of a long driveway. The entire complex was surrounded by a high wire-mesh fence, at each corner of which was a gate with a large security post.

As I got closer I could pick out the maze of antennas on the roof of the administrative building, which led to the communications center which was probably in the basement.

The parking lot in front of the complex was filled with a motley collection of cars and a few buses which belonged to the employees. At the rear of the factory, however, was the production parking lot which was always nearly filled with row after row of *Moskvitch* sedans and coupes—probably the worst constructed cars anywhere in the world.

The only reason they ever sold any of their automobiles was because of the price. A new sedan, fully equipped, could be purchased for around two thousand dollars American, which was a thousand dollars or more cheaper than any other car. The losses the factory incurred were underwritten by the Soviet government, probably as a budget line on the KGB's books.

The factory's main gate was set back at least a half a mile from the highway at the end of an exit ramp. As I passed it, I could see that there was no activity there, although one of the guards was clearly visible leaning against the gatehouse.

Behind the factory complex was the suburb of Machelen, which I headed for, and by eight o'clock I was seated at a comfortable table in a small *bierstube*, drinking a German beer and waiting for my dinner to come.

Heinzman was obviously the source of the Series 700 documents. He probably took them home, one at a time as they were generated by his committee, and made two copies, on one of which he forged Hawk's signature.

I was reasonably certain that the dates on which Heinzman met with the Russian Grechko would correspond with the dates on which 700s documents were distributed throughout the system, to Hawk as well.

Heinzman would return the original set of documents which would be routinely copied and then distributed.

One of the copies he made would go to Grechko; the copy with Hawk's forged signature would later be switched with Hawk's own copies after he had signed them.

That operation, however, raised two immediate questions in my mind: The first was how did Heinzman accomplish the switch once Hawk had signed his set of series 700s; the second was, what became of the set that Hawk had signed once they came into Heinzman's possession?

I knew that one set had been found on the dead courier in Paris. But how about the others? Somewhere there had to be a cache of eighteen months worth—unless Heinzman had destroyed them.

My Wiener schnitzel came and I ordered another beer. As I ate my meal I couldn't help but go over in my mind all the inconsistencies in this case. No matter which way I looked at the facts, no matter which theory I tried to fit them into, my thinking always came up short.

If it was exclusively a Russian operation, how did they find me in my hotel in Paris? Who was the second dead man whose body Burns had seen at the Paris morgue? Who had shot him and why? And if Heinzman was the key, and was working for the Russians, why did they allow him to live in such an obviously grand manner.

On the other hand, if Hawk was the traitor and he had not been the one who had ordered the second body placed in my room to help cover my escape, who had done it? And why?

The only solid fact I had was that Bruno Heinzman, a high-placed member of NATO, had met often with a Soviet representative of the Skaldia-Volga factory. That alone was enough to assure an indictment for treason.

The chain ran from NATO to Heinzman, and from Heinzman to Grechko. There was only one place where I had even the slightest chance of finding out where it led after that. Although I would be taking a huge risk going there, I had no other choice. I was at a dead end.

After I finished my meal I drove back toward the city where I stopped at the Hilton Hotel. From the desk clerk I got a large manila envelope which I addressed to the Director of Operations, Amalgamated Press, Washington, D.C. I stuffed Heinzman's appointments book inside and sealed the envelope, then handed it, along with a twenty *franc* note, back to the clerk who assured me it would be mailed first thing in the morning.

No matter what Mandel personally thought about Hawk's innocence or guilt, Heinzman's appointments book along with the scrap of paper containing Hawk's signature, would have to make him think. Would have to force him into looking very closely at Heinzman's background.

By ten-thirty I was back in Machelen and by eleven I had found what I was looking for: a place to inconspicuously leave my car near the rear approaches to the S-V plant.

It was a parking lot at the rear of a medium-sized office building of some sort. The parking lot was perched at the edge of a steeply sloping field of grass that ran down to a drainage ditch, and then up on the other side to the S-V property fence.

A couple of hundred yards to the right along the fence was a gate, but to the left there was nothing for at least a thousand yards, although there were powerful lights every fifty yards or so along the fence line.

I only had to wait one half hour before a whistle sounded from the factory. Within a few minutes men came streaming out the doors heading for their cars and the buses, while at the gate I could see to the right, the guards were suddenly very busy with the shift change.

I got out of my car, carefully picked my way down
the steep slope to the drainage ditch and then, keeping
low, climbed up the other side to the fence.

The shift change, I figured, would take at least ten or
fifteen minutes during which time the security guards
would be too busy to watch the fence line.

Through the fence, less than ten years away, were
the rows of new *Moskvitch* sedans and coupes. Beyond
them was a railroad siding that ran along the back of one
of the assembly buildings. Several boxcars were parked
at loading docks, but from where I was lying at the
fence I could see no workmen.

The administration building was to my left, around
the corner of the main assembly building, at the front of
the complex. One way or the other I was going to have
to get to it undetected.

I took out the diamond-edged wire cutters from my
tool kit, and although they were small the jaws easily
cut through the fence. Within a couple of minutes I had
opened a hole large enough to crawl through.

On the other side I bent the fence wires back so that
the damage would be invisible, except to close exami-
nation, and then worked my way across the open space
to the concealment of the first rows of new cars.

There was still a jam of cars and pedestrians at the
gate I could see from here, as I quickly made my way
through the parked cars to the railroad tracks where I
ducked under one of the boxcars and came up on the
other side, between it and the loading dock.

I was about to stand up and look over the edge of the
dock, when I heard two men, speaking French, come
outside from the factory and I stiffened.

They were saying something about the weather and I
could smell the odor of strong tobacco. For a full five

minutes they stood talking like that, joking and laughing, until a third man came out on the loading dock and shouted at them, his French heavy with a Russian accent, and the three of them left.

I waited another sixty seconds and then carefully stood up and looked over the edge of the dock, which was about twenty feet wide and led through an open service door into what appeared to be a warehouse loaded with wooden crates.

No one was in sight as I climbed up on the dock and quickly slipped inside the warehouse, where I raced noiselessly to the left down one of the narrow aisles between the stacks of crates.

A whistle blew and a few seconds later I could hear the sounds of heavy machinery starting up deeper within the factory as the late shift began its work.

The storeroom I was in was large, at least two hundred feet long, and beyond the last row of crates was a corrugated plastic service door that was closed, but I could hear a great deal of machinery running as well as men talking and shouting at each other on the other side.

To the right, beyond the door was a metal-runged ladder that led upward toward the high ceiling from which fluorescent lights hung at intervals from the girders.

I shaded my eyes against the glare and could dimly make out what appeared to be a large hatch in the ceiling, which probably gave access to the heating and air conditioning units on the roof.

For a long moment I held my breath, listening to the sounds of the factory. Then I stepped out from behind the stack of crates and sprinted past the service door to the ladder and immediately started up.

I was about fifteen feet off the floor when the service door rumbled open and a man driving a forklift came into the storeroom, turned down the aisle that led to the ladder where I was perched and stopped directly below me, maneuvering his vehicle to a stack of crates that I could have easily jumped down on.

I froze against the ladder, not daring to move or even breathe as the man expertly shifted the stack of crates, removing one of them.

If he had looked up at any time he would have seen me, but when he had the crate he had come for, he backed his machine around, raced down the aisle and through the service door which rumbled closed behind him, and I let out a deep sigh of relief.

At the ceiling I reached up and was about to push the hatch open, when I noticed a pair of thin wires leading away from the hinges and I stopped my hand in midair a couple of inches away.

It was a simple alarm system that would be activated if the hatch was opened. In the dim light I could see the micro switch on the center hinge.

Hooking my left arm around the ladder, I pulled out my tool kit and within sixty seconds I had wired across the tiny switch so that it would always indicate a closed hatch, and then checking once more to make sure I was still alone in the storeroom, shoved open the hatch, crawled out onto the roof and softly closed the hatch behind me.

Seen from here the factory appeared much larger than it had from the highway. The irregular roof line was huge and seemed to stretch forever in every direction.

Quickly I raced toward the middle of the building so there would be less chance of being spotted from the ground. Keeping low, I headed toward the administration building, nearly a thousand yards away, that jutted well above the factory, much like the bridge on a huge ocean tank ship.

No lights shone from any of the windows on this side of the administration building, nevertheless I approached it with extreme caution, ducking behind air vents, air-conditioning units and other protuberances, until I was within a few yards of a door that opened onto a metal-runged porch. A ladder was attached to the side of the building, next to the door, providing access, I supposed, for the antennas on the roof.

I hurried across the open space, climbed up over the railing onto the porch and quickly searched the doorframe for any sign that it too was wired for an alarm. But I found nothing and within a few seconds I had the lock picked and was easing the door carefully open.

A wide, dimly lit corridor stretched the length of the building, with office doors on either side at regular intervals.

I slipped inside and picked the lock of the first door and let myself into a small office that contained nothing more than a desk and a couple of file cabinets. A chart of some kind was pinned to a cork wall that was filled with what appeared to be work orders.

Quickly I went around the desk and looked through the drawers until I found the S-V telephone directory in which Grechko was listed as an administrative officer in charge of trade relations. His office number was 407.

I took out my Luger and slipped the safety off before I eased open the door to the corridor and stepped out. This had been too easy so far, and I was getting jumpy.

Heinzman had to know that I had taken his appointments book. He also had to assume that I understood the significance of Grechko's name. If he had told the Russian about me, there would have been more security here.

The fourth-floor corridor was a twin of the one I had just left, and within a minute I had found 407 about halfway down, had picked the lock and had slipped inside.

Grechko's office was much larger than the one I had entered downstairs, his desk larger, a bank of file cabinets built into one wall. A leather couch, coffee table and two solid-looking easy chairs were grouped near the wide window and a Picasso print hung on the opposite wall. It was a far cry from other Soviet offices I have been in; nowhere here did I see the standard picture of Lenin. Nor could his office be termed austere in any sense of the word.

I looked at my watch which showed it was quarter after twelve. My entry had taken forty-five minutes, and with luck I would be able to leave the same way; in much less time.

The next shift change would take place around seven in the morning, I figured, and no one would be here in the administrative building until then.

I had the entire morning to come up with the next link in the chain and, although I didn't know exactly what I was looking for, I felt certain I would find something.

TEN

I had found nothing of interest until well after four in the morning, but then I hit the jackpot. Grechko's desk had contained little of value except for a set of powerful binoculars and a 35 mm camera fitted with infrared lenses. Nor had I come up with anything in his extensive files under the headings Heinzman, David Hawk, AXE or NATO.

By one o'clock I had exhausted all the routine possibilities, and had resigned myself to looking through every one of his files, beginning with the first folder in the first drawer of the first cabinet.

Many of the files contained sales reports from all over Europe, some of them in Russian, but the bulk in French or German.

Other files contained parts orders and other instructions from the main offices in Leningrad and Moscow.

Still others contained hundreds of letters from angry customers unhappy with the performance of their *Moskvitch* automobiles. In one series of correspondence, an attorney general from Antwerp had threatened legal action against S-V unless a fleet of sedans sold to a small pharmaceuticals company were either fixed or replaced. The exhaust systems in each of the eight automobiles had fallen off the car onto the highway within the first month of purchase.

Grechko's replies in each case were smooth, showed good business judgment and a sense of apology for the shoddy product he was selling.

If Grechko performed no other service for the Soviet government, I remembered thinking at one point, he was doing a damned fine job selling cars and keeping people happy.

But then I came to a series of files each containing the dossier of a man or woman who worked with or for S-V. Or at least that's what the files appeared to be until I came to the dossier on Yuri Ivanovich Noskov, the dead courier in Paris on whose body the Series 700 documents had been found.

His file indicated that he worked as an engineering consultant for S-V, on loan from the parent plant in Moscow, but another sheet marked, FOR NEWS MEDIA DISTRIBUTION, indicated that he was a financial consultant for the embassy here in Brussels.

Stamped across Noskov's file were the red letters M.D., with Grechko's signature at the bottom. ''M.D.'' were the letters which stood for the Russian words *Mokrie Dela*—which meant wet affair, the KGB terminology for assassination.

I stared at the file for a long time in the dim light coming from the window. Noskov had been set up. His death had been no accident. The files with Hawk's signature on them found on his body had been planted, obviously to incriminate Hawk. It had been an Ouster conspiracy after all.

But what else? I was sure there was something else.

I took out four other personnel files at random and compared them with Noskov's file, immediately noticing that the index number in every case except Noskov's, began with either an A, B or C. Noskov's began with a GB.

There were at least two hundred personnel files and I quickly looked at the index number on every one of them, coming up with only four others carrying the GB designation, which I extracted from the drawers and took over to Grechko's desk, along with Noskov's file.

Except for the *Mokrie Dela* notation on Noskov's file all five men could have been the same person, their backgrounds were so similar. They all had been assigned officially to the S-V within two weeks of each other, eighteen months ago. They all were listed as engineering consultants for the factory and financial consultants at the Soviet Embassy here in Brussels.

Each of them had been issued A passports, which meant they could travel back and forth from Russia unhindered by routine Soviet paperwork.

On the same date that Noskov's assassination had been ordered, however, the other four men had been reassigned for "government duty" in Moscow.

From NATO to Heinzman, from Heinzman to Grechko, and from Grechko to five Russian engineers—one of whom was dead, the other four of whom had returned to Moscow.

Why had they killed Noskov, and why had they sent the others back?

Each of the dossiers gave the man's background, as well as his family situation and residence in Moscow. I quickly copied this information down on a slip of paper from a memo pad on Grechoko's desk, and then replaced the files in the exact slots I had found them.

With this new information, plus Heinzman's appointments book, Mandel would have to at least entertain a reasonable doubt about Hawk's complicity. He would have to go to the President with this new information, Hawk could be re-called and with his help we would be able to trace down the actual document flow. How, for instance, Hawk's copies were lifted from him and who was running it. The KGB was a sure bet, but I had no solid proof as yet, although it was possible that AXE's archives would be able to identify one or more of the four names on my list.

At the door I stopped long enough to critically survey the office, making sure I had left everything as I had found it. If they knew I had been here they would have a chance to cover their tracks before Mandel had time to order an operation against them.

Satisfied I had left no indications of my search, I carefully opened the door and slipped out into the still deserted corridor, hurried to the stairwell and went down to the second floor.

The corridor here was empty as well, and within a minute and a half I had let myself out the end door and was back on the factory roof racing toward the warehouse hatch.

Once I got away from here I would telephone Mandel and tell him to expect Heinzman's appointments book and what I had found here. While he was doing his checking in Washington I would stick around Brussels. I wanted to have a word with Grechko.

The night was warm and I was sweating by the time I reached the hatch, got down on my knees and opened it. Two dozen men were working below in the warehouse, stacking crates that were being off loaded from the boxcar outside on the siding. It was nearly five-thirty, and in an hour and a half the day shift would be coming on duty. But before then the sun would be up, and then I would have no chance of escape.

The edge of the roof was about a hundred feet away. Keeping low I hurried to within ten feet of it, and then went the rest of the way on my stomach. I carefully eased myself forward the last few inches and peered over the edge. There was a large overhang so that I was less than fifteen feet away from the boxcar and around five or six feet above its roof. Below me on the loading dock I could see a half a dozen men removing heavy crates from the boxcar by hand and stacking them on pallets so that the forklift trucks could bring them inside.

I was about to pull back when one of the workmen spotted me. Our eyes met and locked for a moment, until I jerked out of sight. Any chance of getting in and out undetected had just gone down the drain. Now it was going to be touch and go whether or not I got out at all.

I jumped up and pulled out my Luger, snapping the safety off, as I raced back to the hatch and flung it open.

''Here,'' I shouted down into the warehouse, firing three shots into one of the crates directly below me.

A siren started wailing as I turned and raced head-long to the edge of the roof and jumped. The fleeting hope that I had not miscalculated the distance briefly flashed across my mind, as the roof of the boxcar came up at me incredibly fast.

I landed badly, lost my balance and almost fell over the edge, but then scrambled to the end of the boxcar where I half-slid, half-tumbled down the ladder.

I had wracked my right knee in the jump, but I

ignored the pain as I raced away from the railroad siding and threaded my way through the rows of new cars toward the fence.

If I could get through the hole I had cut and down the slope I didn't think anyone from the factory would shoot at me. They would not want to create that kind of an incident. Or at least I hoped they wouldn't.

Other sirens were wailing now throughout the factory complex as I reached the last row of new cars and dropped down to one knee.

To my left, a half a dozen guards armed with automatic weapons had assembled outside the back gatehouse. To the right, three more armed guards had just turned the corner and were heading directly toward me.

Keeping as low as possible I scrambled away from the protection of the parked cars, crossing the open space to the fence line in less than five seconds, but they had spotted me.

"Halt! Halt!" I could hear someone shouting from my left.

I found the hole I had cut in the fence and ripped the wires back as the first shots were being fired at me, kicking up the dirt about ten feet away.

Before I crawled through the opening I turned and snapped off two quick shots toward the gatehouse. As the guards scrambled for cover, I dove through the hole in the fence and was rolling and crawling down the slope toward the drainage ditch.

Before I hit the bottom they were firing at me again, but then I was in the ditch, out of sight from the fence line for the moment.

The water was about ankle deep and as I huddled there trying to catch my breath, I wondered just how badly they wanted me. Badly enough to risk an incident with the Brussels police by shooting me when I crawled up the opposite slope to my car in the parking lot?

Already, I was sure, the police had been called by someone and were on their way here. If I was arrested by them it would be a simple matter for the Russians to have me killed.

I took a deep breath, let it out slowly and then started up the opposite slope, crawling and scrambling as fast as I could go, every muscle in my body tense as I waited for them to open fire. But nothing happened. At the top, I turned around in time to see the guards hurrying back to the gatehouse and a large black Mercedes sedan racing through the rear gate.

In the distance I could hear the sounds of police sirens, but within a few seconds I was behind the wheel of the Alfa and pulling out of the parking lot. Heading away from the factory, I was careful to keep well within the speed limit as I worked my way through the Mechelen suburb, finally picking up one of the main arteries that led back into the city.

I had parked the car in the shadows behind the office building, and I was reasonably certain that no one from the factory could have seen its make or color, so I figured I would be relatively safe for the moment. But I cursed my bad luck. It would have been so much simpler if I could have gotten away from the factory undetected. Sooner or later the hole in the fence would have been discovered of course, but I had counted on at least twenty-four hours head start.

Heinzman had probably already skipped and within a few hours Grechko would be on a plane for Moscow. With them gone any hope I had of proving Hawk's innocence beyond a shadow of a doubt would be gone as well.

I needed Grechko to tell me that this was a KGB operation and to fill in the missing details, such as how his people had found me so quickly in Paris.

Without him, Hawk and I were back in the same mess we had been before. Heinzman was the conduit, but Grechko had the answers we needed.

The sun was just coming up behind me when I pulled off Highway 5 to an Esso Station near St. Ulricks west of the city. While the attendant was filling the Alfa's tank, I went into the men's room where I cleaned up as best I could.

The half-healed knife wound in my left shoulder was throbbing, my right knee felt almost as if it was broken and the image staring back at me in the mirror was that of a drunk who had been on a ten day binge.

I was tired, I was running out of money, I wasn't sure if my passport under the name of Morgan was good any longer and I definitely had worn out my welcome in Brussels without accomplishing what I had set out to do—clear Hawk's name.

When I was finished in the men's room I went back to my car, paid the attendant and then continued south-west in the general direction of Paris, as I tried without luck to think this thing out, to make some sense of it.

From the very beginning there had been a nagging doubt at the back of my mind that I was missing something vital, some thought, or clue, or connection that would allow everything to fall into place.

I had felt it in Washington, I had felt it again after the bombing of my hotel room in Paris and again this morning as I ran away from Brussels.

Toward what, I asked myself. Where was I going now? There was nothing left for me in Brussels or

Paris. There was certainly nothing to be gained by returning to Washington, D.C. So what would my next step be?

Burns, my one link with AXE and NATO, was now dead. And the only four people left on this earth who would help me if I asked, were useless now.

Hawk was holed up in a cabin in the Adirondacks, Sandry Triggs was being watched, I didn't want to involve the Countess any further than I already had and Kazuka Akiyama was two continents away from me.

I had often been in tight situations in which I had to rely solely on my own abilities, but never had I felt the crushing sense of aloneness that gripped me as I drove through the pleasant Belgium countryside toward nowhere.

Always before there had been David Hawk, who when all else failed, was an island of sanity for me. A safe haven of absolute trust and understanding.

In Washington, Paris and Brussels I had been on the move, I had been heading in a positive direction and I had not had time to think about myself.

Now that I had nowhere to go, now that the threads had been severed, I found that I was filled with self doubts and the black forbidding thoughts that everything I had ever done in my life amounted to nothing.

I was frightened and the realization was like a continuous low voltage electrical shock to my system.

I came into Mons, a town of about thirty thousand that was less than ten miles from the French border, about 8:30 A.M. Without realizing what I was doing, I pulled off at a small restaurant and parked the car out in the open on the main street.

A half a block away it was market day in the square

and already housewives were haggling with the men and farmwives at the various fruit and vegetable stalls for the best bargains.

I got out of the car and shuffled into the restaurant where I took a seat by the front window so that I could sit in the sun and watch the people in the square. I was the only customer at the moment.

When the waitress came from the backroom it turned out that she was a pretty young girl in a brightly colored skirt and blouse. *"Bon matin, monsieur,"* she said in a sweet voice. *"Café?"*

"Oui," I said tiredly, *"et cognac."*

"Cognac?" she asked, surprised.

I didn't bother to look up. *"Oui,"* I repeated.

She left and a short time later returned with my order, a troubled expression in her eyes. Evidently people in Mons did not drink cognac in the morning.

I looked up at her and smiled. "I've been up all night," I said in French.

She nodded, slight understanding coming to her expression, and she was about to turn and leave when I stopped her.

"Is there a telephone here that I can use?"

"Oui," she said, pointing behind the counter.

"I need to make a telephone call to the United States," I explained. "A very important call. I will pay for it."

If she was surprised by my request she didn't show it. She just nodded her head and pointed again at the telephone.

I stood up and took my cognac with me across the room to the telephone. When I had the overseas operator, I gave her the number at Hawk's cabin and asked her for time and charges once my call was completed.

As she connected with the trans-Atlantic trunk I turned, took a sip of my drink and looked out the window at the people on the square. They fascinated me at this moment because all of them seemed happy and all of them had a place to return to. They all had homes and families.

The overseas operator had connected with the Utica, New York operator and a few moments later the telephone was ringing.

Herbert Mandel answered the telephone on the fourth ring. "I know it's you Carter and I want you to come in," he said, and before I could say anything or even hang up, he hurried on. "Listen to me before you run again, and listen close."

I said nothing, my numbed brain trying to make some sense of this. Mandel at Hawk's cabin?

"David Hawk is dead. He confessed everything before he shot himself."

I heard a noise behind me, and I half turned in a daze as the young waitress rushed across the room to me and grabbed my right hand in which I held the shattered remains of my cognac glass, my blood already starting to drip on the floor.

"Come home Carter. It's all over. Do you hear me? Hawk is dead. He was the traitor. Just tell us what flight you'll be on and we'll meet you."

ELEVEN

I was back at the table by the window, a fresh cognac in front of me and a bandage on my right hand without really knowing how I had gotten there.

The young waitress was hovering over me and two other women who had evidently come from the back room stood around clucking solicitously.

"It is too bad when a young man loses his mother," one of the women said.

"Yes, but it is even worse when he learns of her death in this fashion," the other one said.

I looked up as a large, rotund man wearing a long blue apron came from the counter and handed me a slip of paper. "It came to seventy-eight *francs, monsieur,*" he said.

Confusion evidently showed on my face, because the man tapped the paper with a blunt finger. "Your telephone call, the charge was seventy-eight *francs.*"

"Oh yes," I said, the fuzz clearing slightly from my brain. As if in a dream I reached in my coat pocket, withdrew my wallet, pulled out a hundred-*franc* note and handed it to the man who took it and started back to the counter.

"You can take him upstairs Maria. The gentleman can wait there," he said over his shoulder.

Something in what the man had just said clicked in my mind and I blinked. "Wait for what?" I called after him and he turned around.

"I spoke with your brother on the telephone after your terrible news. He told me that you were very close to your mother, and he was very sorry for breaking the news of her death to you that way."

I pushed back my chair and got unsteadily to my feet, the young waitress helping me. "What else?" I snapped.

"*Monsieur*?" the man said.

"You said I was supposed to wait upstairs. For what?"

"Oh . . ." the man said. "Your brother told me it would be best if you did not travel now. I gave him our location. He said he would send friends down from Brussels to fetch you. Not to worry."

It was like someone had thrown a bucket of ice water on me, everything was suddenly back in harsh focus, and I stepped away from the table. Hawk was dead and now they wanted me.

"Thank you for your concern," I said, trying to keep my voice as even as possible. "But I will drive up to Brussels."

The waitress started to object, but I cut her off.

"No, really, I thank you for your concern, but it will be best if I leave for Brussels this moment. You understand, don't you?"

The girl nodded uncertainly. "My apartment is upstairs, *monsieur*. It would be no trouble for you to rest."

"*Merci*" I said to her. "If I miss my brother's friends tell them I have returned to Brussels and will see them there."

"As you wish, *monsieur*," the man with the apron said. "But if you will wait just a moment I will get your change."

"That's all right," I said backing away from the table and heading for the door. "It is for my drinks, the glass I broke and for your trouble."

I turned and in a couple of steps was out the door, not quite catching what the man was saying to me as I was leaving. I forced myself to calmly cross the sidewalk to my car, slip in behind the wheel and start the engine. The man and the three women had come out of the restaurant and were watching me as I pulled away from the curb, and they were still standing there as I turned the corner at the end of the block skirting the market square and headed for the main highway toward Paris.

Mandel was very efficient and would be moving fast now. With the AXE communications center for his exclusive use, he would have first contacted our office in Brussels which was less than twenty-five miles from here, to send as many people after me as possible. Next, figuring I'd probably recover and run before they got to me, he would have called the DST counter-espionage office in Paris which had responsibility for France's border crossings, with my description. It would take time, however, perhaps as long as a half an hour or more, before that message got to the crossing at Valenciennes where I was heading now.

I made the nine miles in slightly under six minutes

arriving at the frontier at 9:07, taking my place in line behind three cars and a truckload of chickens.

The cars were allowed through quickly, but the customs officials seemed to be having some kind of trouble with the driver of the chicken truck, who stepped down from the cab and began screaming at them in French.

I watched for about five minutes and then got out of my car and walked toward them. One of the customs men broke away and came over to me.

"Sorry, *monsieur,*" he said, coldly eyeing my somewhat disheveled appearance. "It will be just a few minutes."

"I've had car troubles," I said, taking out my passport and my wallet. "I've cut my stupid hand, I've gotten my clothes dirty and unless I have the Countess' car in Paris within the next couple of hours I will probably be shot by her husband."

The official glanced at the car, then took my passport and studied it for a long moment.

"You say it is not your automobile, *monsieur?*" he asked looking up.

I shook my head. "Unfortunately no. The poor woman is dreadfully afraid of her husband. We were in Brussels together when she found out the man was returning to Paris sooner than expected. She had to fly back. Meanwhile there is the car and me."

"Have you the papers for the car?" the man started to say, but I opened my wallet and took out a hundred-*franc* note, which left me with less than three-hundred-and-fifty *francs* and fifty American dollars.

I held out the money to him. "This would pay for a telephone call to the Countess at her home outside the city. She will confirm ownership."

The customs official glanced quickly over his shoulder at his partner who was still engaged in a heated discussion with the trucker then turned back to me, snatched the note from my hand and stuffed it in his pocket. "Have you anything to declare?" he asked handing back my passport.

"Nothing," I said.

"The purpose of your visit to France?"

I smiled. "To assure the return of this automobile, thus saving a marriage, as well as my life."

The customs man smiled and nodded. "Affairs of the heart," he said knowingly. "You may proceed. And good luck."

"Thank you," I said, and as I was getting back into the car another man stuck his head out the doorway of the customs house.

"Lebel," he called, and the official who I had talked with turned around.

"*Moment!*" he shouted.

"It is headquarters," the man in the doorway shouted. "They must speak with you immediately."

"Coming," the customs man said, but by then I had started the car, eased it around the truck, and the striped barrier was being raised for me. I forced myself to drive slowly until I was out of sight of the crossing, then I jammed the accelerator pedal to the floor.

They would be expecting me to head directly for Paris. Once in the big city it would be relatively easy to lose myself and it could take them several days or longer to catch up with me.

All their efforts, I figured, would be directed toward Paris and the highways that led into the great city.

A few miles away from the border crossing, however, I turned off the main highway and headed north. This was a heavily industrialized area of France, and

hotel room, plus a host of other crimes, including the murder of Heinzman's bodyguard.

I stared at the slip of paper, then stuck it in my pocket. I could either run and hide, or continue with the case, I thought as I started on my lunch. Hide or continue. It was as simple as that.

For just an instant I had a very sharp, clear image in my mind of Hawk. He was looking at me, a gruff expression on his face, and shaking his head.

I had no real choice. But when this was over Mandel would be made to account for Hawk's death. And then I would get out of the service.

After lunch I walked around the corner to the telephone exchange building and gave the operator two numbers I wanted to call; the first in Hamburg and the second in Tokyo.

I was assigned a booth and when I had slipped inside and picked up the phone the first number was already ringing. It was answered immediately.

"Hello, Hotel Inter-Continental," a man's voice said in English, but with a very heavy German accent.

"I want a single for tomorrow night," I said. "I'll be coming later in the afternoon."

"Yes," the man said. "The name please."

"Morgan. Mark Morgan."

"Passport?"

"American."

"Yes sir, we will hold a room for you."

"Also," I quickly added, "I will be expecting an American Express wire for a rather large sum of cash, could your people arrange a currency exchange for me?"

"Naturally, *Herr* Morgan," the man said with more deference in his voice. "What currency would you wish?"

"Swiss *francs*," I said.

"It will be arranged, *mein Herr*," he said crisply. "*Aufwiedersehen.*"

The telephone exchange operator broke in when I was finished with the Hamburg call to tell me that it would be two hours before my call to Tokyo could be completed.

I left the booth, paid for my one call at the desk and told the operator I would return in two hours, which would be two-thirty here and eleven-thirty at night in Tokyo.

A half a block away I stopped at a men's clothing store where I purchased a pair of trousers, a pullover shirt and a light jacket. And at a luggage shop across the street I purchased a medium-sized imitation leather suitcase with a bright paisley cloth lining.

Finally I took a cab across town to the railroad station where in the men's room I changed clothes, stuffing my old, dirty clothing in the suitcase which I then checked in a pay locker before I purchased a one-way ticket to Hamburg, a second class, on the overnight train which left at seven this evening.

All that had taken less than an hour, but it left me with only fifty dollars American and an assortment of less than thirty *francs,* French and Belgium.

The next step was as dangerous as it was necessary. I was going to have to get rid of the Alfa. Already, I was sure, there was an alert out for the car which would have been identified by the customs official who had let me through at Valenciennes. If the local police here in Lille discovered it in the carpark, it would be a simple matter for the authorities to trace my movements to Hamburg, and probably the call I was going to make to Tokyo later this afternoon.

In addition I was going to need a new passport to get

across the border; the Morgan passport would be useless here in France. And I needed at least a small
amount of cash on which to travel.

Outside the depot I selected the shabbiest looking
cab and got in the back seat. The driver was an old,
decrepit looking man. He was smoking a Gauloise, the
butt hanging insolently from his lip at the corner of his
mouth. I help up the American fifty dollar bill.

"*Oui monsieur?*" he said, hungrily looking at the
money.

"A friend of mine wishes to sell his automobile very
fast. No questions asked. Who should he see?"

The old man's eyes widened. "*Non,*" he said, but I
waved the fifty dollar bill a little closer to his nose.

He hesitated a moment longer, but then snatched the
money from my hands, turned forward and crashed the
car in gear and took off. "Rochambard," he said half
under his breath.

Ten minutes later we were on the other side of town,
in a very seedy neighborhood, where the driver pulled
up across the street from an auto salvage yard.

A large wooden sign over the driveway said
"ROCHAMBARD'S," but the place looked deserted.

"Behind the fence there is a truck. Rochambard's
office is there."

"I hope you have not lied to me, *monsieur,*" I said
ominously, and the old man blanched and shook his
head.

I got out of the cab and before I was all the way across
the street, the driver had driven away, crashing gears as
fast as he could make the cab go.

There was absolutely nothing of value in the small
junkyard, and how anyone could have made a living
here was impossible to conceive. Yet when Rochambard answered my knock on the door cut into the back

of an old Mercedes truck, he turned out to be a man in his late fifties, dressed in a fine Italian silk suit, spotlessly clean white, tailored shirt, and what appeared to be Gucci loafers. I figured the cabby had not lied to me after all.

"*Monsieur* Rochambard?" I asked.

"You're an American?" the man said in English, his voice soft and obviously cultured.

"Yes," I said, "and I need your help."

"Come in, come in, I'm sure you can be accommodated."

Inside, the truck had been decorated to match the man's appearance, with soft lighting, thick carpeting and a few items of expensive furniture including a marvelous old leather-topped desk.

He started to pour me a drink, but I waved it off. "I have very little time," I told him.

"So," he said turning back to me. "You are on the run. You need a passport to get out of the country immediately. You are in such a hurry that you do not care about its quality or previous ownership, so long as it will get you where you wish to go. And you are willing to pay well."

I smiled. "Plus I need five-hundred dollars in cash."

The man laughed out loud. "It is you who must pay me, not the other way around," he said, but then his eyes narrowed. "Unless you have something of obvious value in exchange?"

"A new Alfa Romeo Spyder."

"You have the papers?"

I shook my head, and his expression darkened. "It is an expensive automobile, but there are certain expenses I would incur in dealing with it," he said half to himself. Then he looked up. "Where is this automobile?"

I told him the name of the carpark.

"And when must you have your passport and money?"

"Before six o'clock this evening."

"Difficult," he said, again half to himself.

"Fine," I snapped, and I turned toward the door, but the man quickly stopped me.

"Difficult, I said, but not impossible."

I turned back, pulled the keys and the carpark check out of my pocket and tossed them to him. "I'll need one hundred dollars now. The rest plus the passport at the Café Tremaine on the square by six."

"You've given me only keys, and you want a hundred dollars?"

"Yes," I said nodding. "A little trust on both sides."

The man laughed again, but he pocketed the keys and carpark check, took out his wallet, extracted four, one-hundred-*franc* notes, and handed them to me. "I do not like to be cheated, *monsieur*. I have connections with the local police."

"I don't like to be cheated either," I said pocketing the money. "I would kill you."

Rochambard nodded. "Then we understand each other," he said. "Six o'clock then. But you must understand that the passport I will provide on such short notice will not be very good. Only an approximate likeness and age."

"That's fine," I said, and I turned and left his truck.

I had to walk eight blocks before I finally found a cab and by the time I got back to the telephone exchange I was five minutes late.

The operator was a little angry because she had held the line for me, but I apologized with a bright smile and she assigned me a booth.

A few moments later I was speaking with a very surprised Kazuka Akiyama at her apartment in Tokyo.

"What in heaven's name is going on Nick?" she shouted over the long distance line. "The office has been getting directives almost hourly that you are to be shot on sight. What have you done?"

"Is your phone clean?" I asked.

"Of course . . ." she started to say, but then cut it off. "Just a moment."

A few seconds later she was back. "My phone is clean, now what is going on? What have you done?"

I had been prepared to hang up immediately. I did not want Kazuka involved in this mess, and yet I had no one else to turn to.

Quickly I recounted for her everything that had happened to me, and everything I had learned since the man at the Washington airport had tried to kill me.

Through the telling she was absolutely silent, but when I was finished she was angry and deeply shook.

"Mandel is ruthless, but he'd never order Hawk's elimination," she said.

"He told me himself," I countered.

"I'm coming there," she answered after a moment. "Where are you?"

"No Kazuka, you are not coming here. The moment you left Tokyo they'd be on to you. But I do need your help."

Kazuka was a pro and she understood immediately that I was right. "What can I do?"

"I need some money. Twenty thousand dollars American."

"Where and when?"

"You'll have to blind drop it through American Express for me from the States, in the name of Mark Morgan. I'll be at the Hotel Inter-Continental in Hamburg tomorrow afternoon. I'll have to have it by then because I won't be staying there long."

"That's a lot of money, Nick. What are you planning?" she asked.

"I can't tell you, Kazuka. But you must trust me."

"I love you Nick, are you forgetting?"

"No," I said softly.

"I'll get on it right away," she said after a moment. "And good luck."

"Thanks. I'm really going to need it this time."

TWELVE

By six o'clock I was standing at a newspaper kiosk across the square from the Café Tremaine, and as the clock on a nearby church tower began striking the hour, Rochambard pulled up in a black Chevrolet, got out and went into the restaurant.

The newspaper stand was run by an old man and his young grandson, and I turned to them now and held out a five-*franc* note to the boy.

"Would you like to run an errand for me?" I asked.

The boy looked up at his grandfather who nodded, and then turned and took the money from me. "*Monsieur?*"

I pointed across the street to the Chevrolet. "The man who owns that car is in the restaurant. He will be coming out in a moment. When he does I want you to tell him to walk to the Telephone Exchange where the man with the car will be waiting."

The boy nodded and hurried across the street as I went around the square and took up position two doors away from the telephone building.

Rochambard showed up a couple of minutes later, alone, and went into the building.

When he came out I was standing by the doorway, and when he saw me he broke into a wide grin. "Never too careful, heh?" he said coming to me and extending his hand.

I shook it. "You have the money and the passport?"

"Yes," he said, and he withdrew an envelope from his pocket and handed it over. "I have the car. It is a fine automobile."

I slit the envelope open, pocketed the sixteen hundred *francs* and looked at the passport. It was for a Robert Wilcox, Bear Run, Pennsylvania, whose photograph showed a somewhat overweight man in his early forties, with a brush haircut.

Rochambard had not been kidding when he had told me that the likeness would not be good. But it would be night and I hoped that the Belgian and German border people would not be too alert.

"It was the best we could do, *monsieur*, on such a short notice," Rochambard said, watching me. "If you could wait perhaps a day or two?"

I looked up and shook my head. "It will be fine as long as there isn't a warrant on this man."

"I assure you, *monsieur*, this document is clean. It was taken some months ago in such a way the owner believed it was merely lost."

I hailed a cab which had just pulled around the corner, and it stopped at the curb.

"If there is anything else . . ." Rochambard said trailing off as I got in the cab, but I ignored him, and told the driver in a loud voice to take me to the airport.

As soon as the cab had gone around the corner, out of sight of Rochambard, I canceled my previous instruction and told the driver to take me to the train depot instead.

The driver shrugged his shoulders, and within five minutes I was deposited in front of the depot where I went inside and retrieved my suitcase from the locker.

If Rochambard was going to pull a double-cross on me, he'd go out to the airport. And by the time he figured out that he had been duped, I'd already be gone.

I didn't really think the man would pull such a stunt, but I could not be sure. I was going to have to be very careful from this point on.

At the counter I purchased a first-class ticket to Hamburg. When it was time to board the train, however, I got on the second-class coach showing the conductor the second-class ticket I had purchased before.

The train pulled out of the depot at seven sharp, and when the conductor had come around to collect tickets I handed mine over, showing him my Morgan passport. A few minutes later I moved into the first-class coach where I turned over my first-class ticket, showing the official my Wilcox passport.

If they started looking for Mark Morgan at the border, the second-class coach conductor would tell them that I had been on the train, but had evidently jumped. It would keep them busy for a while.

I had a compartment to myself, and as soon as the conductor had left, I took off my shoes and my jacket, lowered the bed and crawled in beneath the covers.

The train crossed into Belgium near Roubaix which was a short ten miles out of Lille, so I had just settled in with only a dim light shining from my bathroom, when the train slowed down and stopped to allow the Belgian authorities to board and check passports.

I did not have long to wait before there was a knock at my door. I counted ten seconds, and then in a sleepy voice told them to come in.

The door opened and two Belgian customs officials came into my compartment and I squinted up at them as I handed up my passport.

One of them checked it, glancing at me twice, but then handed it back. "Sorry to have disturbed your sleep, *monsieur,*" he said. When they were gone, I breathed a sigh of relief.

I threw back the covers, got out of bed, lowered my window and looked outside. To the rear of the train from me, there were a half a dozen men standing around the second-class car. Although I could not hear what they were saying, from their gestures it appeared as if they were having an argument. One of the men was the conductor who had taken my ticket, the others were all Belgian customs officials.

The Belgian authorities had been notified after all and were looking for Morgan.

I ducked back into my compartment, closed the window and sat down on the edge of the bed, my hand on the grip of my Luger concealed beneath the covers.

There was a possibility that they would search the train, not believing that the man from second class had jumped, but twenty minutes later the train pulled away from the border crossing and I was on my way back to Brussels, and from there to Dusseldorf in Germany and finally up to Hamburg.

The German authorities would not be looking for me unless Kazuka was caught trying to wire me money, or unless Rochambard was caught with the Alfa and was made to reveal my new passport.

There were too many ifs there, and instead of getting

some much needed rest, I remained awake through the night, only crawling back in bed to feign sleep when we crossed into Germany and the authorities came aboard to check passports even more perfunctorily than the Belgians had.

The train pulled into the *Bahnhof* Dammtor downtown Hamburg shortly after seven in the morning. After exchanging the rest of my French *francs* for German *marks,* I took a cab across the Alster on the Kennedy Bridge and checked in at the Hotel Prem, using the Wilcox passport.

From my room I telephoned the Inter-Continental, identified myself as Mark Morgan and asked if my American Express money wire had arrived yet. The clerk assured me it had and the hotel would change the money order into Swiss *francs* later in the morning.

I cleaned up and left the hotel shortly before ten, where I found a men's clothing shop at which I purchased a suit, a fresh shirt and a tie. At a luggage shop around the corner I purchased an inexpensive attaché case.

Back at the hotel I changed clothes and, with the attaché case in hand, took a cab back across the Alster to the Hotel Inter-Continental where the obsequious manager had me sign two documents, studied my passport and then carefully counted out the pile of Swiss currency that he had personally exchanged from the twenty thousand dollar American Express money wire.

As I was stuffing the money into my attaché case, the hotel manager asked if I would require the room at the hotel that I had reserved.

"Naturally," I said, looking up at him. "I will be staying in Hamburg for several days on business. I'll have my bags sent over later this afternoon."

"Very good, *Herr* Morgan, we look forward to serving you."

I locked the attaché case and got up from where I had been sitting across from the manager. "I've been expecting some business aquaintances to meet me here in Hamburg," I said. "Has anyone asked for me last night or this morning?"

"No sir," the clerk said. "Would you care to leave a message?"

"No," I said. "If someone does ask, you may inform then that I will be back to the hotel late this afternoon."

"Very good, *mein Herr*," the manager said, coming around his desk and showing me to the door.

I took a cab back to the Hotel Prem where I paid for a full week, and at one of the guest writing desks in the lobby I grabbed a half a dozen hotel envelopes and then went up to my room.

After I had divided the money into the six envelopes, I telephoned the Lufthansa and made reservations for the late flight to Washington, D.C., under the name Morgan, and then left the hotel.

My first stop, shortly before noon, was at the train depot where I purchased a first-class ticket on tomorrow evening's train to Paris, under the name Wilcox. Before I left the depot, however, I tore the ticket up and scattered the pieces amongst several trash bins.

Next I stopped at five banks in quick succession exchanging my Swiss *francs* into Finnish *markkas*, leaving the one envelope with its money intact.

By two o'clock I presented myself at the downtown

Hertz office, where I filled out the necessary forms and paid the deposit on a Porsche, under the name Morgan. I told them that I would be driving to Berlin and would be back in one week.

By two-thirty I had stopped at another luggage shop where I purchased an expensive leather suitcase with a thick cloth lining. Then, two doors away at a fabric store, I picked up a small sewing kit and finally headed south out of the city on the E4 toward Hannover ninety-five miles away.

Between the two names, the two hotels, my reservations with Lufthansa and the train ticket to Paris, I figured it would keep anyone looking for me busy for at least a few hours, and hopefully longer.

But I wanted to muddy the trail just a bit more before I actually left Germany.

It was just four o'clock when I pulled into the carpark at the airport north of Hannover and eased the Porsche into a slot in the long term parking area.

It would be several days before anyone began asking questions about the car, I figured, which would give me more than enough time to do what I had to do.

I took a cab into town from the airport, where at the *Bahnhof* I purchased a first-class ticket to Copenhagen, which left in two hours, giving me plenty of time for dinner.

On the train I was going to sew my weapons and most of the money into the lining of my suitcase, and after a night in a Copenhagen hotel, I was going to fly on to Helsinki, where I figured I would have at least thirty-six hours, if I was lucky, before they caught up with me.

All during the long day I had been busy and had not had much time to think. But waiting for the train as I picked at my dinner in a small *Bierstube* near the depot, I kept seeing David Hawk sitting on the end of his dock in the Adirondacks.

His death was so senseless. He had devoted his entire life in the service to his country and his reward had been death at the hands of his own people.

Someone was going to pay for it, I thought grimly. Someone was going to pay heavily.

I had been to Helsinki twice before in my life, the last time nearly seven years ago when I had been assigned to help a defector coming out of Russia to make his way to the United States.

It had been a bloody affair that should have taken less than twenty-four hours, but instead had dragged on for nearly three weeks.

During that period I had gotten to know a certain portion of the city fairly well and had made the aquaintances of a number of underworld figures, among them Jätk Toffolii, who at the time was a very old man, but one of the best forgers in the business. He was tolerated by the Finnish government and the Helsinki Special Branch Police because of his raging hatred for the Soviet Union. The unspoken policy was that as long as Toffolii did not create too much of a fuss in Helsinki he would be left to his own devices.

I checked into a hotel just off Kalevankatu, a few blocks away from the Finnish National Opera House, about four in the afternoon. After I had taken a leisurely shower, I went downstairs and had an early dinner and a couple of drinks. The attaché case went into the hotel safe, minus two of the five envelopes of Finnish currency, which I stuffed in my jacket pocket.

By 7:30 that evening I was ready, and although I had to appear to be nothing more than an ordinary tourist who was not in much of a hurry, I had precious little time in which to get what I needed and then leave the city before I was recognized.

I took a cab to within walking distance of the city's waterfront district along the South Harbor, where I entered one of the rougher seamen's bars, where seven years ago Toffolii had done business.

At the bar, which was crowded with men and a few hard-looking women, I ordered a beer and sat quietly minding my own business for a half an hour.

When my second beer came, I paid for it with some change and then laid a twenty-*markka* note on the bar. "If a man wanted to find Jätk Toffolii, where would he go?" I asked softly.

The bartender laughed, but he scooped up the money and pocketed it. "That's an easy one. Old Jätk is less than two kilometers from here, where he's been for the past two years."

I knew what was coming.

"He's about two meters underground, just behind the Old Church on Lönnrotsgatan. For another twenty I'll give you directions."

No one else in the bar was paying any attention to us, but as I pulled out a hundred-*markka* note and laid it on the counter, the barman's eyes widened perceptibly. I had caught his attention.

"Jätk was a good man," I said softly. "A professional."

The barman nodded, his eyes on the money. "A true expert."

"I had hoped to do business with him," I continued. "Big and very expensive business. But quickly."

The barman looked up into my eyes. "Travel papers," he said, his voice so low I could barely hear him, but I nodded.

"I'm going east."

The barman blinked, and then very slowly reached down and took the hundred-*markka* note off the bar and placed it in his pocket. "Wait in a booth," he said, nodding toward the back of the bar. "A man will come to you in a few minutes."

Without another word I slipped off the stool and took my beer to a back booth where I sat down and lit myself a cigarette.

I did not have long to wait before a thin man with a very large nose and ears, dressed as an ordinary seaman, joined me. He appeared to be in his early twenties.

He reached out and took my cigarette from my fingers and puffed deeply on it before he handed it back. "You were inquiring about my father?"

My eyebrows rose. "I didn't know Jätk had a son."

"He didn't," the little man said, smiling. "But I was his son from the age of maybe four or five. I learned from him. In his last years I was his eyes and fingers. He depended upon me. And now you are seeking help."

"I want to go to Moscow," I said. "But I am known there by the KGB."

It was the little man's turn to raise his eyebrows. "Difficult, and very dangerous for all of us. The State Police are very efficient," he said. "What would you do in Moscow?"

I wondered briefly just how much of a son this man had been to Toffolii. "Kill Russians," I said evenly. "They have killed two of my friends."

The little man slapped his right palm softly on the table top and grinned, showing a mouthful of black, rotten teeth. "My politics are on your side *Amerikaner*, but it will cost you much, nevertheless."

"I'll need the documents within twenty-four hours—no later. And I'll also need a car. I will drive to Simola before I take the train."

The little man nodded his approval. "It will be possible for you if you stay only overnight in Moscow. No longer. By then you will be identified as an imposter and will be arrested."

"That gives me plenty of time," I said.

"Are you willing and able to pay well?"

I nodded.

He gave me an address of an apartment building directly on the waterfront just a few blocks from this bar and told me to check out of my hotel immediately.

"Tell them you have been unexpectedly called away from Helsinki, then bring yourself and your money to my home. I'll be waiting for you."

THIRTEEN

There were a number of reasons, I suppose, why I had become careless; I was too intent on the next step of my plan and I had lulled myself into a false sense of security with the belief that it would take AXE and the CIA at least thirty-six hours to catch up with me.

Whatever the reasons, however, I did not pay much attention to the man in a dark business suit who was standing in the corner of the busy hotel lobby watching me as I went to the desk.

Nor did I pay much attention to the fact that the desk clerk seemed uneasy when I asked him to prepare my bill and get my attaché case out of the hotel safe.

"I've been called out of town suddenly," I said, "and I have to leave this evening."

"We're sorry to hear that, Mr. Morgan," the man

said. ''When you are ready with your things, your bill
will be prepared.''

''I'll get them now,'' I said, and I turned and went
across the lobby to the bank of elevators thinking about
the little forger. I hoped that he would be at least half as
good as Toffolii, who had been a master.

When the elevator came I punched the button for the
fourth floor and, as the doors slid closed, I noticed that
the clerk was now speaking with the man in the dark
suit who had come across the lobby to the desk, yet I
still attached no significance to it.

On the fourth floor I hurried down the corridor,
checked to make sure my door had not been tampered
with and then went inside where I quickly grabbed my
suitcase.

Less than four minutes had elapsed from the time I
had entered the busy hotel until now as the elevator
doors slid open and I stepped out into a nearly deserted
lobby. Alarm bells began jangling along my nerves, but
without breaking stride I went across to the desk where
I set my suitcase down.

The man in the dark suit was seated, reading a
magazine on one of the couches. Across the lobby a
bellboy was at his station intently studying a guest
register, and near the door a maintenance man was
doing something to one of the hinges.

It was a setup, I could feel it thick in the air as I rang
the bell for the clerk who popped out of the office
behind the counter a second later with my attaché case
in hand.

The clerk laid the case on the counter and I opened it.
The envelopes of Finnish currency were still there, and
I shut and re-locked the case, then paid the bill the clerk
presented me with.

I didn't think the forger had turned me in, he stood to

lose too much money. The only other explanation was that they had a worldwide alert out for me and field men in every capital had been watching the airports, docks and depots. I must have been spotted at the airport. During the couple of hours I had been absent from the hotel they had set everything up for me.

I grabbed the attaché case and, in a voice loud enough so that everyone in the lobby could hear me, I told the clerk that I had forgotten something in my room.

As I turned and started away from the desk, the man in the dark suit looked up, the bellboy turned around and the maintenance man at the door swiveled my way.

An instant later I swung around, and in two quick strides was back at the counter where I leaped over to the other side on top of the startled clerk.

"Stop him!" one of the three men in the lobby shouted, and as I ducked below the level of the counter-top a shot was fired, slamming into the wall over my head.

Without hesitation I scrambled on all fours through the door behind the counter and slammed it shut as four more shots were fired in quick succession.

Leaping to my feet I raced across the deserted office and out the door on the other side, finding myself in a narrow corridor that led left to a heavy metal door with an exit sign in Finnish illuminated above it.

They'd be waiting for me in the alley, I was sure of it, so I just stepped aside, away from the office door. I had to find out who they were. If they were CIA, AXE or Finnish police, I could not return their fire, no matter what the circumstances. But if they were Russians it would be a different story.

A moment later the door swung open and the man in the dark suit came barging through. I stepped to the

right, shoved him aside and slammed the door behind
him as he tried to bring his pistol around.

An instant later I kicked out with the toe of my right
shoe, catching the side of his left knee and, as he started
to collapse, I smashed my fist into the side of his head
and he was out.

For a long second I held my breath, listening for the
sounds of pursuit, but the hotel was quiet. Quickly I
bent down, flipped open the man's suitcoat and extracted his wallet. Inside was a plastic, U.S. Embassy
card identifying him as Charles Brodley. The only
people in any U.S. Embassy who carried weapons
besides the Marine guards, were CIA personnel.

Brodley was a local case officer, which meant I had
been spotted at the airport by his people.

I threw the wallet down and eased the office door
open; the room was still empty. When I had leaped over
the registration desk, they had probably directed most
of their people to the back of the hotel. But they would
not stay there long.

Across the office I carefully looked around the
corner out into the lobby. There was no one there. But
that was the way they did things. Clear everyone out so
that if there was shooting no innocent bystanders would
get in the way.

I stepped out of the office behind the counter, sat up
on it and swiveled around to the other side, where I
quickly went to the main doors. Outside were a half a
dozen cars parked in the street. Several men stood
around, weapons in hand. One of them was speaking
into a walkie-talkie. At each corner, either way down
the street, were Finnish police cars, their blue lights
flashing.

Away from the door I turned and raced across the
lobby into the cocktail lounge where the clerk who had

given me my attaché case, the bartender and a couple of cocktail waitresses were seated at the end of the bar.

They all looked up, frightened, as I barged in and withdrew my Luger. I pointed the gun in their general direction.

"Everyone out!" I snapped. *"Now!"*

They got down from the barstools and started for the cocktail lounge exit to the street, but I waved my gun toward the lobby. "Out the main doors!" I said.

They stopped, confused, for a moment.

"Move it!" I ordered urgently. "Or I'll kill everyone of you!"

They scrambled past me and out into the lobby where they went out through the main doors.

I turned, rushed across the lounge and eased the outside door open a crack just as two men who had been watching the exit raced around to the front of the hotel where I could hear a great deal of commotion going on.

I reholstered my Luger, stepped outside and, unchallenged, turned left and walked away from the hotel, keeping to the shadows as much as possible.

The police car at the end of the block was deserted and I walked past it unnoticed. Within a couple of minutes I was around the corner on the busy Albertinkatu where I hailed a passing cab and ordered him to take me to an address about two blocks away from the forger.

As the cab pulled away from the curb, I looked out the rear window in time to see two police cars race around the corner from the hotel and speed past us.

I had escaped their net and now they knew it. Within a few hours they would be turning this town upside down looking for me.

It was a short drive across town down to the South Harbor area, and ten minutes later I had paid the cabby and headed on foot to the address the forger had given me, which turned out to be a large, rather nice apartment block.

The night was cool, and nearby I could hear the sounds of water lapping against the pilings, the smells of cordage, tar and the sea, and an occasional ship's whistle as she steamed into the harbor.

I had been given only an address and an apartment number on the first floor, not the man's name. I mounted the steps to the building, opened the front door and went inside.

Except for the dim light in the entryway that shone on the rows of mailboxes set into one wall, the corridor was in darkness.

For a long moment I hesitated just within the doorway and then I stepped to the mailboxes, where I found the apartment number the forger had given me. On every other mailbox there was a name card. On his there was nothing but the number: 121.

I started to turn around toward the dark corridor when the little man spoke to me from the darkness.

"I have a gun on you and I'll shoot, unless you turn around and leave here immediately."

I tried to spot him, but could not. "What's the trouble?" I asked softly. From one of the apartments down the corridor I could hear a radio or a television playing, and there was the smell of cigarette smoke drifting toward me.

"There is big trouble with the police, Carter," he said. "You are a wanted man. I cannot help you."

"I can't leave Helsinki without travel papers," I said, slowly holding up the attaché case. "Whatever figure you had in mind, I will pay double."

"Go," the man said, but with less certainty in his voice than before.

"I have no quarrel with the Finnish authorities. I want to go into Russia. I have an old score to settle."

"You cannot stay here," the man said.

I took a step forward so that I was slightly out of the light. "Then get me out of the city. Tonight. There must be someplace we can go to in the country where it is safe. Where you can make my papers."

The forger was silent for several long seconds and, holding my breath, I could hear his faint breathing down the corridor. He was less than ten meters from me.

I was about to speak again, when he said, "I would have asked for ten thousand *markkas*. Can you pay twenty thousand?"

"Yes," I said. I had nearly fifty thousand *markkas*. "I have the money with me." I raised the attaché case a little higher. I was taking a chance; he could kill me right now and steal the money. But I didn't think he was a murderer. "I'll pay you a bonus for your extra expenses, as well as for the car."

The little forger appeared from down the corridor, a troubled expression on his face as he pocketed an American military .45 automatic. "The car will not be necessary," he said. "My sister lives in Simola. I will take you there tonight where I will do your documents and get ready for your journey to Moscow."

"You called me Carter," I said. "Where did you hear that name?"

The forger smiled, but the gesture was devoid of all friendliness. "Your name and description are being broadcast on all the police channels. You are a traitor."

"I am not," I said. "I'm being framed."

The forger chuckled. "They all say that. Frankly I don't care as long as you kill Russians. I will see you on the train to Moscow tomorrow, or the next day at the latest, and then I will wait for your return. If you are not back within twenty-four hours plus the time of the train ride each way, I will tell our police where you have gone. They can deal with it from that point.''

"Jätk knew me and helped me once seven years ago,'' I said.

"I know,'' the little man told me. "It is the only reason I will help you now.''

Simola was a tiny town less than ten miles from the Soviet border, well above the Gulf of Finland. It had been carved out of the dense coniferous forest that stretched unbroken two hundred and fifty miles north to the Arctic Circle, and beyond to the beginning of the tundra. Its only industries were sawmills and one pulp factory which shipped rough products by rail to Lahti in the west and Helsinki in the south.

Simola was the final stop in Finland before the rail line crossed into Russia, and the forger, whose name was Karl Hakkala, passed the railroad depot housed in a long, low wooden building before he went to his sister's home on the edge of town.

"You will have no trouble here in Simola,'' the little man said. "Although you will be getting on the train here, your ticket will be stamped from Helsinki, with the return portion for two weeks from now.''

"I can only stay overnight.''

"I know,'' Hakkala said impatiently. "I will give you another return ticket for the next day. It will show that you entered the Soviet Union two weeks earlier. I will also give you a second set of travel documents. The first will remain at your hotel. There will be less questions this way. For instance: Why would a man merely take a train ride into Moscow one day and leave the next?''

We had left Helsinki last night around midnight in Hakkala's battered Simca sedan, with me huddled in the trunk until we were several miles out of town.

The hundred and twenty-five mile trip was made in darkness, and we traveled through dense forests so I could see little of the countryside.

It was still dark when we pulled up behind his sister's house, which was a small, shake-roofed bungalow, with tiny latticed balconies beneath each window on the second floor. The house was dark.

We got out of the car and crossed the yard in a bitterly cold north wind that took my breath away. Before we mounted the steps onto the back porch, however, Hakkala turned to me.

''My sister is very young, very beautiful and is a widow. If you so much as look wrong at her I will not hesitate to kill you.''

''I have a job to do,'' I said. ''I'm here for travel papers, nothing more.''

Hakkala looked into my eyes for a long moment, then shrugged, mounted the steps, knocked once on the door and went inside.

''Ursula,'' he called from the dark kitchen. ''It is Karl.''

A moment later a woman's voice came from the head of the stairs. ''Karl?'' she called. Then she said something in Finnish that I couldn't quite hear, and her brother replied and nodded his head.

He went to the kitchen window where he shut the curtains and then turned on the light over a small table around which were four chairs. He motioned for me to sit down.

"Are you hungry?" he asked.

"A little," I said. I sat down, laying the attaché case under the table at my feet.

Hakkala looked at it and smiled. "I am a forger, not a thief, Carter. I will not steal your money."

I was about to say something when his sister came downstairs and the words were choked off in my throat. She was easily the most beautiful woman I had ever seen in my life.

She was wearing a bright orange quilt robe clutched at her throat, her feet encased in down slippers. But her hair was light blonde, almost platinum, and fell down her back nearly to her waist. The pale, delicate skin of her face, with high cheek bones, tiny chin and full lips, perfectly framed her wide, dark eyes.

She stopped at the kitchen door, evidently surprised to see a stranger sitting in her kitchen, and she turned to her brother and said something in Finnish, her voice soft and lovely.

Hakkala seemed irritated. "Do you speak anything other than English, Carter?" he asked.

I had not taken my eyes off his sister. "French, German, Italian, Spanish, a little Japanese," I said.

"*Permettes-mois de tu présenter* Nick Carter," her brother said.

"*Enchanté*," the woman replied and I nodded. "What brings you to Simola *Monsieur* Carter," she asked in French.

"I have business with your brother—" I started to say, but Hakkala cut me off.

"He is on his way to Moscow to kill someone," he said. "He needs travel documents."

A startled expression crossed the woman's face, but then she smiled. "Are you a dangerous man?" she asked me.

"Ursula!" Hakkala snapped, and she turned to him as he rattled off a stream of Finnish.

She nodded when he was done, and without looking at me, crossed the kitchen where she began taking food and dishes from a cupboard.

Hakkala sat down at the table across from me. "We will have breakfast and then start immediately on your documents. I want you out of here soon Carter, very soon."

FOURTEEN

It was a quarter after ten at night and a gentle snow was falling as I waited by the car for Hakkala who had gone inside the depot to speak with the station master.

The train now on the tracks was scheduled to depart at 10:35 P.M., and would arrive tomorrow afternoon at four o'clock in Moscow. I had return tickets for the next morning's train back to Simola.

I had seen a lot of forged documents during my career with AXE, but I had to admit that Hakkala's were the best I had ever come across—including those of old Jätk's.

Passport, driver's license, credit cards, social security number and Soviet work permit, resident card and travel documents, all identified me as Robert Eklund, vice president in charge of Maintenance Operations for the John Deere Farm Equipment Company. All the documents looked well-used and authentic.

He had given me two suitcases in which we had packed some spare clothing and a large supply of sausages, coffee, sugar and small canned hams.

"It's quite common for American businessmen assigned to Moscow to bring in such food items," Hakkala had explained. "They are all the things impossible to find in Moscow stores, and your fellow employees at John Deere would expect you to bring such presents. For the border patrol people who will search your luggage it would seem strange if you did not carry such contraband. They will probably charge you a stiff import duty, but they would surely stop you for a strip search if you did not carry such things."

He came out of the depot a couple of minutes later, nodded and, without a word, helped me with the two suitcases from the trunk.

Before we went around to the waiting train, he looked critically at me, and then nodded again. "It is the best I could do on such short notice," he said. "But it will work."

I was dressed in an American business suit over which I wore a fur coat, thick fur-lined boots and a Russian mink hat.

Hakkala had shaved the top of my head and thinned out the hair at the sides, dying it totally white. I was given a white mustache, thick-lensed glasses and was instructed to walk with a heavy limp.

Ursula, using a professional stage makeup kit, had changed my facial appearance so drastically that I appeared to be a man easily in my sixties, with dark bags beneath my eyes, slack skin around my cheek bones and a few thin blue veins here and there.

A few dozen people were saying their goodbyes on

the platform, and as Hakkala led me limping to the first-class car he gave me my final instructions.

"Just across the border the train will stop for a Soviet crew and for your customs check. You will have to get off and stand in line with your suitcases. Leave your weapons aboard the train."

I looked sharply at him. "If I run into trouble there, what then?"

Hakkala smiled. "You won't," he said.

I nodded, but said nothing.

"You will have from sixteen hundred tomorrow until zero seven hundred the next morning in Moscow to do what you must do. I'll look for you back here by twenty-two hundred that night."

We had come to the first-class car where we stopped and Hakkala looked up into my eyes. "If there is any trouble, Carter, and you are not back on the twenty-two hundred train the day after tomorrow, I will assume you really are a traitor and go to the police. I'll tell them you are in Moscow."

"Thank you for your help," I said, but Hakkala turned and started back toward his car. I watched him until he was around the corner, and then turned and boarded the train, showing the conductor my ticket.

"Compartment Six-B," the man said.

"Will I be sharing it with anyone else?" I asked.

"No sir," the conductor said. "On this trip you have the compartment to yourself."

I thanked him, found my compartment and let myself in, wondering if he or anyone else on the train were friends with Hakkala and knew that I would be trying to get across the border on forged papers.

It was likely, I thought. But I knew that I could not count on them for any real help if I ran into trouble at the check point. I would be on my own.

I set my suitcases down by the door and then went to the single window and looked outside. Hakkala had driven his car down the road a few yards so that he was parked across the station yard from my compartment, but he was looking in the opposite direction, and after a moment I shut the window curtain and pulled my bed down from where it folded into the wall.

I slipped off my coat and withdrew my stiletto with which I made a small slit in the bottom side of the mattress. Into this hole I stuffed my Luger and the extra clip of ammunition that Hakkala had supplied me. I was about to shove my stiletto in after it, but then decided against it, returning the knife to its chamois sheath beneath my coat sleeve.

If there was going to be trouble at the border I wanted at least a chance of survival. The gun would have been too easy to find even in a casual search. But I would have to be stripped in order for them to find my stiletto or gas bomb.

Before I allowed that to happen, however, I would first fight my way out of there.

At exactly 10:35 P.M., a whistle sounded two short blasts, the train began moving and my stomach tightened in a knot.

This was my last chance to clear Hawk's name. I was taking a huge risk going into the Soviet Union and there was a very good chance that I would never get back out alive. But I was taking another risk as well. I was gambling that the four men whose names I had found in Grechko's files would be at the addresses listed, that they would know something that would help, that they would tell me and that they would not be under surveillance as many KGB operatives were when they returned home from a foreign assignment.

I had no other choice though. I had run out of options. There was nowhere else for me to go to find the answers I needed. Was this a Russian operation after all? And was David Hawk involved with it?

I shoved the bed back up into the wall and stood there a moment, my hand on the latch, thinking about Hawk. For most of my adult life I had worked for him. I had known him, loved him and sometimes even feared his wrath. But I had never doubted him. Nor had I ever told him how much respect I had for him. It was just not the kind of a thing you said to Hawk. And now it was too late.

Shaking my head in frustration, I turned away from the bed, went into the tiny bathroom and flipped on the light over the mirror.

An old man stared back at me from the mirror, but I could still feel the woman's touch on my face. Ursula had supplied me with a couple of sticks of touch up makeup disguised as styptic pencils, and had instructed me to keep my hands away from my face lest I ruin her work.

So far the makeup had held up fine and I figured I would not have to do anything to it until it was time to get off the train in Moscow. If I got that far.

I turned off the bathroom light, went back into my compartment and at the window drew the curtains aside again and looked out.

We had just come out of a line of trees and were crossing a wide field, the snow falling much harder now. And in the distance ahead I could see strong lights illuminating a tall guard tower, below which was a wire-mesh fence.

It was the Soviet border.

A few minutes later the Finnish conductor was outside my door shouting, ''Soviet border, Soviet border, have your papers and baggage ready for customs.''

As I pulled on my fur coat I could hear the man shouting the same instructions farther down the car, and then the train lurched and began to slow down.

I opened my compartment door, hefted my suitcases and went out into the corridor, along with several of the other first-class passengers who were already heading toward the end of the car where the conductor was waiting with his own suitcase.

Apparently a train heading west, back into Finland, would be waiting on a siding so that the crews could switch.

When the train finally came to a complete halt, the conductor opened the door, lowered the step and jumped down, helping his passengers down one at a time.

I was sixth in line, and when I stepped down to the conductor he pointed to a small wooden building at the base of the guard tower, and said, ''Customs check that way sir,'' in a loud voice. Half under his breath, he quickly added, ''Good luck. We'll see you the day after tomorrow.''

But then the next person behind me was stepping down to the gravel alongside the train and I was limping along toward the customs shed where a half a dozen armed Soviet guards were closely watching the approaching passengers.

Inside the shack it was stiflingly hot, and I had to wait nearly ten minutes before it was my turn at one of the counters, where an old, fat woman in a bedraggled uniform held out her calloused hand to me.

I laid my two suitcases up on the counter, took my papers from my breast pocket and handed them over.

Quickly and efficiently, the woman flipped open my passport, checked it against my Soviet papers and then motioned for me to remove my hat. When I had, she looked up at me and then back at the passport photo several times before she motioned for me to open my suitcases.

Carefully I undid the leather straps on both cases and flipped open the lids. The woman went through the things, holding up two of the canned hams for the clerk at the counter next to hers, and they both laughed.

"He looks well heeled, should be worth a hundred at least," the man said in guttural Russian. I had thought it best not to tell Hakkala or his sister that I also spoke Russian.

The woman turned to me. "There will be a heavy import duty on these food items," she said in Russian.

"I'm sorry I don't understand," I said in English. "*Nyet.*"

The woman laughed. "You will have to pay import duty for this food," she said in English.

I nodded and pulled out my wallet, showing a thick wad of Finnish currency, withdrew three hundred *markkas* and held it out. "Will this be enough?" I asked innocently.

The woman's eyes had gotten larger and the clerk at the next counter over was grinning. "Yes," the woman said taking the money from me. "It will do."

She stamped my passport and Soviet travel permit and then handed my papers back to me. As I stuffed them into my breast pocket and put my hat on again, she tagged my suitcases.

"You may return to the train," she said.

A couple of minutes later I had my suitcases buttoned up and was back outside limping toward the first-class compartment, past a long line of second- and third-class passengers who still had to go through customs. It would take at least another hour, I figured.

Back in my compartment with the door locked, I breathed a deep sigh of relief, got undressed, pulled my bed down and crawled beneath the covers.

Before I went to sleep, I pulled my Luger and extra clip of ammunition out from the hole in the mattress and shoved them under my pillow.

I was in Redland. And in sixteen and a half hours I would be in Redland Headquarters. Once I was there I would have barely fifteen hours to do what had to be done, and not get caught.

As I drifted off I thought about Ursula, and the last thing I was aware of was my curiosity about what she would look like with her clothes off.

I came half awake when the train finally began moving again, but then fell sound asleep a few minutes later. Twice during the night I woke up. Once when the train was stopped for some reason and once to go to the bathroom as we passed through some tiny town.

Outside it was snowing in earnest and the heat vent over my door was cold. For the Russians, heat evidently was an unnecessary luxury.

I was awake by 8:30 A.M., and the sun was just coming up, brightly in the east, reflecting sharply on the freshly fallen snow. The sky was totally cloudless and the heavily wooded countryside looked fresh and lovely, but very cold and uninhabited.

I had just gotten out of bed and was dressing, when someone knocked on my door and I stiffened.

"Yes?" I called out.

"Mr. Eklund, it is the conductor, may I speak with you?" a man's voice speaking English asked.

I went across the room, unlocked the door and

opened it. A tall man, in a conductor's uniform stood looking down the corridor. When he turned to me he seemed nervous and his eyes widened slightly.

"Mr. Eklund?" he asked.

I nodded sleepily. "Yes? What is it?"

"May I come in?"

I held the door all the way open and stepped aside as the man nearly jumped into my compartment and quickly closed the door.

Something was going on and I tensed ready for a fight. "What do you want?" I asked, keeping my voice neutral.

He stared at me a long moment and then glanced over toward my suitcases. "I would like to purchase your coffee and sugar," he said breathlessly.

I smiled, relaxing.

"I will pay well for it," he said. "But I have only *rubles*." He reached in his coat pocket and took out a wad of Russian money. "It is for my wife you see. She likes her coffee with sugar. And I—"

I cut him off. "Of course," I said. I turned and went across the room where I set one of the suitcases up on the bed and opened it. I took out a large can of coffee and a two kilo package of sugar and handed them to the man.

"How much do you want?" he asked, nervously.

I shook my head. "I do not know their Russian value. You may pay me whatever you think is fair."

The man seemed to think a moment, then he peeled off several of the larger bills and handed them to me, a questioning look in his eyes.

I took the money. "This is fine," I said. "I hope your wife enjoys her coffee."

"I thank you for her," he said. "But may I ask one additional favor?"

I nodded.

"Say nothing about this to anyone. Please."

"I won't," I said, and I moved toward the door as he stuffed the coffee and sugar beneath his coat. But before I could open it, he stopped me.

"A piece of advice, Mr. Eklund," he said softly.

We were less than two feet apart and he reached out and touched my cheek.

"If you are to leave this compartment for meals, first fix your makeup."

My blood ran cold, but I nodded, and a moment later he turned and went out the door.

I locked it after him and went into the bathroom. The makeup around my eyes had smudged and a wide black smear ran from my left cheek down to my neck.

Working very carefully, it took me ten minutes to repair the damage I had caused in my sleep. When I was finished I looked slightly different than before, but still passable and still close enough to my passport photo to pass any but the closest of inspections.

I had just put my things away when someone knocked at my door again. "Yes?" I said.

"Mr. Eklund, it is I, the conductor again."

I opened the door and the man came in. He was carrying a package wrapped in brown paper, which he handed to me. "I have brought you some vodka, some meat, some cheese, some bread and a small tin of caviar."

"I was going to the dining car."

The conductor shook his head. "There is an officer of the State Security Police in the dining car. It would not be safe for you."

I started to say something, but he held me off.

"It is of no concern to me that you are coming into my country illegally. I have no love for the State Police.

No one does. And I have as much to lose as you do. If I
am caught with the coffee and sugar my entire family
and I could go to prison for a very long time." He
smiled sadly. "It is best you remain here in your compartment until we reach Moscow. After that . . ." He
shrugged his shoulders, letting the sentence trail off.

I had no choice other than to trust him. "Thank
you," I said. "May I pay you for the food and drink?"

The conductor shook his head. "It is not necessary.
Be careful."

"Thanks," I said again, and the man turned and left.

I locked the door after he was gone, set the package
he had brought me down on the bed and went to the
window where I pushed the curtains back.

Sometime during the early morning hours we had
passed through Leningrad and the train was now heading southeast toward Moscow. We had come out of the
pine forests and were traveling through farming country, the already harvested fields a bland checkerboard
of browns and muddy blacks half covered with snow.

Occasionally in the distance I could see the onion
dome of a church or some other building, and from time
to time the train paralleled a paved highway. But there
was no traffic.

Shortly before noon I opened the package the conductor had brought me, ate the food and drank a little of
the vodka which was quite mild and very good.

Later in the afternoon I took apart my Luger and put
it back together again, and then took a short nap,
waking with a start around three from a dream in which
Mandel was holding a loaded revolver at Hawk's temple.

I could feel Mandel's finger squeezing the trigger,
but at the instant the gun went off I sat up in a cold
sweat.

In the bathroom I got a drink of metallic tasting water, checked my makeup, which was still passable, and then went back to the window.

The land had flattened out and we were passing through a sparse birch forest. I could see houses through the woods, some of them very large, and there was a small amount of traffic on the highway—mostly farm trucks with an occasional automobile.

We were approaching Moscow and it would not be long now before I was going to have to lay everything on the line.

It was my last chance to clear Hawk. And if I was a betting man, I would not have given myself very good odds for success.

Hakkala had made reservations for me at the Metropole, Moscow's most famous tourist hotel, through a travel bureau in Helsinki. But I had decided during the night that I was not going there.

The hotel would be watched, I was sure. And I would be hard pressed to explain to anyone why I was not immediately contacting my company which had its offices in Moscow.

All it would take was a simple telephone call from someone at the hotel to the John Deere offices asking about a Robert Eklund, and I would be exposed.

I strapped on my shoulder holster, put on my suitcoat and straightened my tie as I thought out what my first moves would be.

If I made a mistake too early in the game, the alert would be sounded and what little chance I had of success would evaporate. It would do no good, I knew, to try and make it back to Finland without the answers I needed. Mandel would spend the rest of his life chasing me. Sooner or later I would make the big mistake, and I was bound to, and he would have me.

If I could find the proof, any kind of proof that this had been exclusively a Russian operation and had nothing to do with Hawk, I could return home and lay the entire thing out for Mandel.

Heinzman, Grechko and whatever I came up with here in Moscow. It would have to add up to innocence for Hawk.

FIFTEEN

The sun was already low in the western sky, casting long shadows as I emerged from the train depot in downtown Moscow. The sky was starting to cloud up again, however, and a bitterly cold wind blew, causing me to shiver involuntarily.

Moscow was a dark, brooding, forbidding city, unlike Paris or Brussels or even Helsinki. It was only shortly after four in the afternoon but already there were signs that everyone would soon be indoors, latches latched, windows locked, outside lights turned off.

I hunched up my coat collar and crossed to the taxi stand where a half a dozen battered Mercedes and *Moskvitch* sedans were waiting. My suitcases were checked in a locker downstairs, and in a shop on the mezzanine of the modern, well-equipped depot, I had purchased a tourist map of the city for a few *kopecs* from an old woman wearing an apron and a babushka.

I climbed in the back seat of the first cab in line, expecting a warm interior, but the cab was just as cold as the outside. The driver turned to me and grinned, most of his teeth missing.

"*Amerikaner?*" he asked.

I nodded and his smile broadened. He turned all the way around in his seat and stuck a huge, calloused paw at me. "Pleased to meet you," he said, his English barely understandable.

I shook his hand and returned the smile. "Happy to meet you," I said.

"Okay," he boomed, "where we headed?"

"Crystal Café," I told him. "Kutuzovsky Prospekt." The restaurant was advertised as Moscow's finest on the tourist map and it was only a couple of blocks away from two of the addresses on my list.

"Good choice," the cabby said, and he turned, ground the gears getting the car into first and we took off in spurts and starts, the driver humming what sounded like a Benny Goodman tune.

I had a brief thought that if all Russians were like the conductor, the old woman in the shop and this cabby, there would be no trouble between us.

We passed by GUM, Moscow's huge, ornate department store near Red Square, and a few minutes later the cabby pulled up in front of the glass-fronted Crystal Café, housed in a grimy building.

I paid him, but he refused a tip, effusively wishing me a pleasant stay in Moscow, and then he continued down the street, the cab bucking and jumping as he ground the gears and raced the engine.

Inside, the place was crowded, noisy and smoky,

and I was shown to a small table off in a corner by myself where I was given a menu.

I ordered a carafe of vodka, some smoked salmon and caviar, along with a dark, very hard bread and a bowl of cabbage soup. All specialties of the house, the young waiter told me.

Most of the people in the place were young Russians, although I was reasonably certain that a few were Americans, probably from the embassy. All of them seemed to be arguing heatedly, some about religion, some about China and others about the Iranian situation. Everyone in the place seemed to be talking at the top of his or her lungs, the reason becoming painfully evident when a five-piece band took its place on a tiny, raised stage and began to play.

They were bad, but they were loud, and soon the dance floor was filled with twisting, gyrating bodies; those who remained at their tables, stomped their feet in time with the music.

I had arrived at the club by five, had ordered, been served and had eaten my excellent meal by six-thirty; by eight o'clock my head was buzzing with the music.

Several young women had come to my table and asked if I wanted to dance, and each time when I declined they merely shrugged their shoulders and went off in search of other partners.

I had gone into the men's room where in one of the stalls I had checked my Luger and had studied the tourist map so that I knew exactly where the first man on my list lived.

At 8:30 I paid my bill and left the club, the cold night air and quiet outside a tremendous relief.

Once again I felt an overwhelming sense of loneliness. The food I had eaten, although quite good, lay heavy on my stomach and my brain was spinning slightly from the vodka. Yet I had a job to do tonight and I was going to have to make sure I did it cleanly, so that tomorrow morning I could leave this place on the train without trouble.

As I headed down the street, walking with a heavy limp, my hands stuffed deeply into the pockets of my fur coat, I wondered just what kind of information I was going to be able to extract from the four men on my list.

The first was Yevgenni Aleksandr Aladkov, forty-four, a bachelor who lived at 1207 Pitkin Place. Like Noskov, the dead courier in Paris, he had been listed in Grechko's files both as a financial consultant with the Brussels embassy as well as an engineer with S-V.

A trolley bus with a brightly lit interior and only a few passengers rumbled by as I reached the corner and crossed the street to a wide, cobblestoned square at the center of which was an ornately carved statue of a man on a rearing horse.

In the square I stopped a moment and looked down each of the four intersecting streets. As far as the eye could see there was no traffic, nor was there even one pedestrian. Only a few lights shone from most of the buildings, and for a moment I had the feeling that I was in the middle of a huge, deserted city. The war had come and the people had either left or had been killed, leaving behind only the dark streets.

The feeling made the biting wind feel even colder and I hunched my coat collar up higher as I continued around the statue and down the narrow street marked Pitkin Place.

A block from the square the street turned left into a cul-de-sac that opened to a wide parking lot surrounding a fourteen-story apartment building. Piles of dirt and mud were everywhere, along with stacks of lumber and bricks. The building had evidently been recently built.

I stopped in the shadows of a storefront at the end of the block and looked across the driveway toward the building. There were a few cars parked in the lot, and in a large rack to the right of the front door were at least four dozen bicycles.

For ten minutes I remained standing, watching the building, the cold penetrating even the heavy fur coat I was wearing, as I waited for some kind of activity. Someone leaving the building. A car coming down the street and into the parking lot. But except for the dim light at the main entrance of the building, and a few lights shining from windows here and there on several of the floors, the place could have been deserted.

I slowly unbuttoned my fur coat and also my suit coat, checked to make sure my Luger was loose in its shoulder holster, and then quickly crossed the parking lot, mounted the four steps and entered the front door.

The building *was* new and smelled of plaster dust, but the odor of cooked cabbage was also strong. A single, unshaded light bulb dangled from the low ceiling over a huge bank of mailboxes set into one wall. A corridor ran straight back from the front door the length of the building and across from the mailboxes was a single elevator, its indicator stopped at the fourth floor.

Silently I crossed to the mail slots and found 1207, on which a small card with Aladkov's name, handwritten, was stuck in a holder.

I had it opened in a couple of seconds with a slender metal pick from my tool kit, but there was nothing inside. After I closed and relocked it, I went across to the elevator and pressed the call button. As the elevator was slowly descending from the fourth floor, I went back to the main door and looked outside. The street was still deserted, although I could hear what sounded like a jet airliner coming low over the city.

The elevator doors slid open and I turned, crossed the lobby and inside the car hit the button for twelve.

It seemed to take forever before the doors slid closed and the elevator started up with a lurch. I watched the floor indicator slowly working its way upward as I took off my fur coat and draped it over my left arm. I wanted my right free for my Luger or stiletto, whichever was necessary.

The doors finally opened on the twelfth-floor corridor which was narrow and poorly lit. I reached over to the control panel and flipped the emergency stop switch. If anyone was going to come up behind me, they would have to take the stairs. When I was ready to leave I did not want to have to wait for the elevator.

Apartment 1207 was four doors down the corridor and from inside I could hear music playing softly. I knocked, then withdrew my Luger, slipping the safety catch off.

The music stopped a moment later and I could hear someone coming to the door. "Yes?" a man said in Russian.

"Comrade Grechko wishes to speak with you," I said, muffling my voice with my hand.

The door was unlocked and, as it started to swing inward, I shoved hard, barging in past a startled little man dressed in nothing more than a pair of slacks, and open neck shirt and slippers.

I closed the door behind me and raised my Luger directly at the man's face as he regained his balance, his eyes wide.

"Are we alone here, Comrade Aladkov?" I snapped.

The man stammered something, but then nodded his head. "Yes—yes, I live alone," he managed to stutter.

I reached back and turned the latch, locking the door, and then motioned Aladkov toward the couch.

The apartment was tiny and consisted, as far as I could see, of nothing more than the sparsely furnished living room, a small efficiency kitchen and, tucked in one corner, a tiny bathroom. One window with no curtains on it looked out over the city. In the distance I could see the domes and spires of St. Basils in Red Square.

"Who are you?" Aladkov said, regaining some of his composure as he sat down.

I draped my heavy fur coat over the arm of the couch, then I brought one of the chairs from his small kitchen table across the room to him and sat down.

Laying the Luger on my lap, I took out a cigarette, lit it, inhaled deeply and then picked up the gun and pointed it in his general direction.

"I am a desperate man, Comrade Aladkov. And I mean to kill you tonight unless I get the answers I came looking for."

The man's eyes widened, but he nodded his head. "What do you want from me?"

"Who do you work for?"

"Colonel Grechko . . . ." he started to say, but then he checked himself. "I mean Comrade Grechko."

"Skaldia Volga Automobile Works, Brussels?"

The man nodded.

"Tell me about Comrade Noskov," I said softly.

The man flinched. "I've never heard the name."

"Bruno Heinzman?"

The man shook his head, his mouth working but no sound coming out.

"Bruno Heinzman?" I repeated. "NATO? Brussels?"

"I don't know," Aladkov said, his voice cracking.

"Bruno . . . Dieter . . . Heinzman," I said slowly, raising the Luger a little higher.

"I don't know . . . I don't know," Aladkov said, his voice rising in pitch.

Carefully I reached up with my left hand and levered the Luger's ejector back, releasing it with a snap, and Aladkov blinked.

"Grechko used to meet with him in town sometimes," he said in a rush. "That's all, I swear it. I don't know anything else."

"What was your job in Brussels?"

The man was beginning to sweat and he ran his right hand over his forehead. "I was a courier, nothing more. I was given papers and other things to bring home in the diplomatic pouch."

"I thought you worked for S-V?" I snapped.

"I did," Aladkov said. "But we . . . I also had courier duties for the Embassy."

"Colonel Grechko," I said. "Colonel in what? The Army?"

"Yes . . . yes, the Army."

"The Strategic Missile Service?"

Aladkov shook his head. "No . . . the Army."

"The KGB?"

Aladkov jerked almost as if he had been slapped. "No," he said weakly.

"What Directorate, Aladkov?"

"The Army," he said, and I leaned forward in my chair.

"Please," he stammered, but I said nothing, and he looked from my eyes to the gun and back to my eyes.

"The KGB . . . all right, Grechko works for the KGB. First Chief Directorate."

I smiled. "What Department?"

"S," Aladkov said, his voice barely audible, but it was like a hammer blow between my eyes.

S was the illegals directorate. S was the department within the KGB that ran foreign deep-cover operations. It was not the department that stole secret documents such as the NATO Series 700s. If Aladkov was lying to me, why would he tell me Grechko worked in the S Directorate? It didn't make sense.

"You're lying to me, comrade," I said.

"No—I swear it—I'm telling you the truth."

"What was Grechko's mission in Brussels?"

"I don't know."

"You *do* know, Aladkov," I said softly, but my mind was spinning in a thousand different directions. "Just as you know about Heinzman."

"Grechko met with him, that's all I know."

I jumped up suddenly and leaped to the couch where I grabbed the man by the front of his shirt and pressed the barrel of the Luger directly on his left temple.

"I'm done playing games with you now Aladkov. Now I want the answers or I'll pull this trigger. *Now!*"

"Heinzmann was supplying Grechko with NATO documents," the man said in a rush. His eyes were wide and saliva ran down from the corners of his mouth.

"Were they signed documents?" I asked.

"No . . . yes," Aladkov said.

"Whose signature?"

"David Hawk's. AXE."

It was like another hammer blow. "What about Noskov?"

"He was given the documents to bring home."

"Why was he killed?"

Aladkov was silent.

"Why was he killed?" I repeated.

"We already had the documents," the man stammered.

It was another hammer blow, although it was the answer I had expected. "Who killed him?"

"I did."

"Why? On whose orders?" I hissed.

"Grechko's."

"Why was he killed, Aladkov? Why were you ordered to kill him?"

"We wanted the NATO documents to be found on his body. We wanted him to be identified as KGB."

"To incriminate David Hawk?" I said.

The man's eyes were nearly bulging out of his head. "Yes," he said.

"One last question," I said, my voice even. "Who set this up? Who was the brains behind it?"

"I don't know," Aladkov said. "I just worked for Grechko."

"Who did he take his orders from?" I snapped, my voice rising.

"I don't know . . . I swear it Carter . . . I don't—" He stopped in mid-sentence, and for a moment I was sure he was going to have a heart attack.

But it was the last hammer blow. *Carter.* He had used my real name. Which meant he knew who I was. He knew I would be coming to Moscow. He had been waiting for me.

"It won't do any good for you to kill me, you know," he said, and I looked down at him.

Hakkala would not have turned me in. Not this soon. But the CIA knew I was in Helsinki, and therefore so did AXE. They could have put it together. They could have figured out that I had come to Helsinki to get into the Soviet Union.

And suddenly it hit me. Everything that had happened finally fell into place. The attempted assassination of me at the Washington airport. The bomb in my hotel room. The extra body. Burns's death. Grechko, Heinzman. Everything finally fell into place.

"We were waiting for you Carter," Aladkov was saying. "We didn't know which of the four of us you'd come to first, or if you'd go to Grechko. But we knew you were coming. We have our people at each of the buildings. My men are downstairs now, waiting for you."

"Then you'll have to come with me," I said. It was now more important than ever for me to get back to Washington. Unless I could stop this operation—totally stop it. The theft of the NATO Series 700 documents would be nothing in comparison to what was possible for them.

I started to move away when Aladkov twisted to the right, in an attempt to knock the gun away from his temple. The movement caused me to jerk and the Luger went off.

Half the opposite side of Aladkov's head exploded, splattering chunks of bone, blood and gray matter across the couch and over the wall ten feet away, and he pitched forward, his eyes bulging and blood pouring from his nose.

I jumped up from the couch and carefully eased the door open. The corridor was still deserted and the elevator doors were still open.

If someone had heard the shot and reported it, they'd be coming up the stairs for me. But they would know that I had switched the elevator off and some of them would be waiting downstairs at the elevator doors for me as well.

For just an instant I hesitated at the doorway, but then stepped out into the corridor and raced down to the elevator, switching the emergency stop off. Immediately the elevator doors closed and the car started down to the lobby.

I stuffed my Luger back into its holster and then, reaching up, shoved one of the ceiling panels out of its track and over, then jumped up, catching the edges with both hands and heaving myself through the opening to the top of the car.

By the time the elevator was passing the third floor I had the ceiling panel back in place and had moved to the light fixture below which was a grate through which I could see the interior of the car.

Past the second floor I withdrew my Luger and tensed. A moment later the car bumped to a halt, the cables twining and rattling high above me, and the doors slid open.

For a seeming eternity nothing happened, but then there was a voice from the lobby.

"He must have sent the elevator down. He's got to be on the stairs."

"He could be on any one of the floors by now, commander," someone else said.

"Switch off the elevator and we'll take it floor by floor," the first voice said.

A young man in a military uniform, a Kashelnikov assault rifle in hand, stepped into the elevator, flipped the emergency stop switch and then left.

I could hear the sounds of several pairs of boots going down the corridor and finally silence.

Carefully I removed the ceiling panel and quietly dropped down into the car. When I had the panel back in place, I stepped to the open doors and looked out into the corridor. There was no one in sight and a couple of seconds later I was outside, the wind even colder now that I had forgotten my fur coat.

There was no movement in the parking lot and still no traffic on the street that led away from the cul-de-sac. Within thirty seconds I had made my way undetected down the driveway and into the shadows of the buildings across the street.

I pocketed my Luger and hurried away from the apartment building, passing the square. A couple of minutes later, I reached the Crystal Café where from within I could hear the raucous music from the five-piece band.

Activity at the club had gotten into full swing, and parked in front of it were several automobiles including one long, black Zil limousine with official plates.

I stood in the shadows across the street from the club for several minutes watching the people come and go. A few feet to the left of the front door a young couple was leaning up against the building, kissing and talking. Father down the block a half a dozen women were smoking and talking with several men.

The train was out. They'd be carefully checking every departing passenger once they discovered I was no longer in the apartment building. My disguise would never stand that kind of scrutiny.

The airline was out as well. For that mode of travel I would need a different set of travel papers. And security at the airport was much more stringent than at the train station.

I stuffed my right hand into my pocket, my fingers curling around the grip of the Luger, and then limped across the street to where the young lovers were standing.

As I approached they turned around to look at me.

"Do you know who owns the limousine?" I asked, nodding toward the Zil.

The young man glanced toward the car, then back at me, and nodded.

"Is he inside?" I asked.

Again the young man did nothing but nod.

"Go in and fetch him then," I snapped, but the young man just stared insolently at me.

I smiled. "There is an emergency at that man's home. If you do not go inside the club and fetch him for me, there will be an emergency right here with you as soon as I call the police."

The young man turned without a word and disappeared into the club while his girlfriend just stared at me.

I turned and limped over to the limousine and after a couple of minutes the young man came back out of the café with another man, much taller and much huskier, dressed in a dark, ill-fitting suit.

The young man pointed toward me and the husky one in the suit hurried down the street my way.

"What is it?" he growled as he approached. "What is happening?"

When he reached me, I withdrew Wilhelmina from my pocket, and holding the gun close to my side for concealment from the young couple staring at us, I said, "You are a dead man, comrade, unless you do exactly as I say."

The color drained from his face. "You are an American," he said.

"Yes. And you and I are going to take a little drive together this evening."

SIXTEEN

We passed Frunze Central Airfield to the northwest of the city on Leningradskoye Road at 10:30 P.M., and a half an hour later were completely away from the city without incident, pounding through the night toward Leningrad itself more than five hundred miles away.

The man whose name was Mikhail Pavlovich Baturin, was a fairly high ranking civil servant in the Moscow Public Works Department and was unarmed. Once he came to realize that I was indeed a desperate man, he gave me no further argument, although he was plainly curious about me.

The enormity of my realization back at Aladkov's apartment had struck me nearly dumb. But now that I had time to think it all out, to examine every aspect of the situation in detail, it all made perfect sense.

I no longer had any doubts about how they had found me so quickly in Paris, nor why Burns had been killed. In fact the only question left in my mind was the extra body in the hotel room. Hawk had evidently set that up. But who had the man been?

Once I got back to Simola I would have to convince Hakkala to provide me with more travel documents. I would not be able to get out of Finland without them.

"Are you a spy?" Baturin asked, breaking into my thoughts.

I turned to him. "No. I came to Moscow to stop some of your spies. They killed a couple of friends of mine."

"Did you kill them?"

"Only one—by accident," I said, wondering why I was telling the man all this.

"And when it is over you will kill me," he said matter-of-factly. "You either have a boat standing by near Leningrad, or you're going to have me drive you up to Vyborg where you will walk through the woods across the border into Finland."

"Something like that," I said. "But no, I have no intention of killing you unless you force me into it."

"I should, you know," Baturin said, and I looked sharply at him as he stared at the road ahead illuminated by the headlights. "I should try to overpower you, or perhaps when we pass through Kalinin or maybe even Leningrad I should attract the attention of the police or the military."

"You would die," I assured him.

"Yes," he replied with a smile. "But so would you."

"Don't back me into a corner, comrade," I said sharply. "Because I may kill you now and figure out some other way to get out."

Baturin shook his head. "The fact of the matter is, Mr.—" he hesitated, but I did not volunteer my name. "The fact of the matter is, I am nothing more than a civil servant and a coward. No, I will give you no trouble."

"What about gasoline?" I asked.

"You are in luck," he said. "I was supposed to drive to Saratov tomorrow so I had the tank filled, and in the trunk there are two twenty-liter cans also filled."

I nodded, and then settled back into the comfortable seat with a cigarette as he raced through the night.

We made Kalinin by about 2:30 A.M., Vyschniy Volochek by six, and Novgorod just south of Leningrad by the time the sun was well up in the eastern sky.

Just outside Kalinin we had stopped briefly so that Baturin could relieve himself at the side of the road, and near Novgorod, in a tiny town, we stopped again where Baturin purchased bread, cheese and two glasses of *kviss*, a terrible tasting citrus drink, and he filled the tank from one of the gas cans in the trunk.

Finally, near one in the afternoon, we entered Leningrad and I began to sweat. If Baturin were planning on making some kind of move, it would be here in the big city where there were plenty of people, plenty of soldiers and a lot of police.

But as we drove into the city from the suburb of Detskoe Seloe, he acted more like a friendly tour guide than a hostage who was helping a self-admitted murderer escape from his country.

"In the west you have Paris and London and New York," he said. "But I have been told that none of your great cities compares in beauty to our Leningrad."

We crossed at least two dozen bridges through the

city, over the Neva River and several canals, passing a grouping of ornately decorated buildings which Baturin told me housed the Soviet Admiralty, built in the early 1700s.

Traffic was fairly heavy throughout the city, and although the day was cloudy and cold, the people all seemed bright and alive. It was quite a contrast from Moscow.

On the north side of the great city we passed through other suburbs that Baturin said once belonged to the Russian nobility. Great houses still stood now containing museums. Vast parks, which had once been the private hunting preserves of the Czars and their families, were laid out in picture-postcard perfection.

It had taken us two hours to pass through the city, and by four Baturin pulled up and parked in front of a small restaurant overlooking the Gulf, in the town of Sestroretsk.

A few people on the village square looked at us in the official limousine, but then averted their eyes as they passed by.

"This is as far as I am able to drive without a rest. If you will trust me, we will go into the restaurant for supper."

The town appeared very peaceful and quiet. The restaurant looked quaint. "And afterwards?" I asked.

"Vyborg is about seventy miles north, the border another fifteen or twenty miles beyond that. I will drive you there and you can drop me off out in the countryside somewhere. I will walk back to Vyborg and tell them what you made me do, of course. But it will give you plenty of time to make it across the border."

"Why are you doing this for me, Baturin?" I asked.

"Would not a civil servant in your country do the same thing?"

"I don't know," I said honestly. "Perhaps not."

"Perhaps not," he repeated. For a moment he stared out the windshield, then he took the keys out of the ignition, opened his door and got out. "I'm going to have my dinner. You may stay here, come with me, or shoot me here and now. Your decision."

I laughed, holstered my Luger and got out of the car as he went around to the restaurant entrance and went inside. We were shown to a small table in the corner by an old man. A moment later a young woman brought us menus.

As I started to look down at mine, I noticed that Baturin was staring at something over my shoulder. I turned in time to see a civil policeman coming across the room, drawing his pistol from his holster.

In one quick motion I shoved the table over on top of Baturin, leaped to one side and withdrew my Luger.

"Don't," I shouted at the cop, but the man kept coming. He had his pistol out and was raising it.

I snapped off a quick shot, hitting the man in the shoulder and spinning him around. The several other people in the restaurant dove for the floor as I scrambled around to the other side of the table and smashed the butt of the Luger into the side of Baturin's head as he tried to get up. He went down like a felled ox, unconscious.

Quickly I grabbed the car keys from his coat pocket, jumped to my feet and raced out the door to the car just as a police car, its blue lights flashing and siren wailing, came around the corner a block away.

I dropped to my knee, waited until the squad car was a little closer and fired two shots. The car swerved to the right and then sharply to the left and crashed into a storefront. I jumped up, got behind the wheel of the limousine, started the powerful engine and raced out of town, the tires burning rubber on the pavement.

I would never know if Baturin had set me up after all. Perhaps he had seen the cop near the restaurant. Perhaps he had not been scheduled to leave Moscow this morning and there was an alert out for him and this car.

Whatever the case, the chances of me making it across the border now had been drastically reduced.

The speedometer crept up beyond a hundred miles-per-hour, and I had to fight with the wheel of the big car in order to keep it on the narrow, rutted highway.

It would not take long for them to sound the alert at the border, and probably at Vyborg as well where they would have the military standing by with roadblocks.

Less than twenty miles down the road I came over a rise and was entering another tiny town with no chance to slow down. I passed four farm trucks in quick succession and nearly ran down a pair of bicylists before I was back on the open highway.

A few miles outside that village, the road split, one to the left following the coastline, and the one to the right going inland. As I went left, I just caught a glimpse of a sign which said VYBORG on the road to the right, and had to slam on the brakes, the car fishtailing back and forth, finally coming to a stop.

I made a quick U-turn on the highway, went back to the inland road and started that way. In my rearview mirror I noticed a farm truck making the same turn, and I suddenly knew how I was going to make it through the roadblocks.

About five miles down the road, I found a narrow dirt path that led off the highway into some heavy brush. I slowed the car down and turned down the path until I was about a hundred yards off the road. Then I forced the car deep into the brush off the path and shut it off.

It would take them a while to find the car, I hoped, and in the meantime I was going to be a farmer going to market—and beyond.

I made it back to the highway a couple of minutes later just as the farm truck I had seen in my rearview mirror was coming down the highway. I stepped out into the middle of the road and flagged him down.

He was an old man, alone in the cab, and when he had the truck stopped, he leaned out the window.

"Are you going to Vyborg?" I asked.

The old man nodded suspiciously. "Yes."

I looked both ways down the road—no one was coming—and I withdrew my Luger. "Down from there," I shouted up.

The old man climbed down from the cab, his hands over his head and, making sure once more that no one was coming, I hustled him back down the dirt path to where I had the limousine parked.

I had him take off his coat and hat, tied his arms and legs with my tie and his belt, and shoved him gently into the back seat.

His coat was a little small for me, but his hat was large and fit well down over my eyes. Back at the highway I climbed up into the cab, eased the truck in gear and started down the road.

The land began to rise slightly and the farm fields began to give way to the dense forests the closer I got to Vyborg, the last Soviet town before the frontier.

About ten miles from the town, a military jeep passed me at high speed, and as I came over the crest of a hill, I could see a pair of helicopter gunships hovering over the highway near the medium-sized city.

Vyborg was in a shallow valley directly on the Gulf of Finland. Beyond the hills on the opposite side of the town was the border.

Between me and there, however, was a bridge which was blocked by a half a dozen military jeeps, a couple of half tracks and the helicopters hovering overhead.

I took a deep breath, made sure the safety catch on my Luger was snapped off—although what good it would do against the firepower they had assembled below was beyond me—and headed down toward the bridge.

Another farm truck filled with manure and straw was ahead of me, but the soldiers at the roadblock just waved the driver through, and then it was my turn as I down shifted, the truck lumbering down the road.

About ten feet from the half a dozen soldiers who stood blocking the road, I leaned out the window. "What is it?" I shouted in a guttural voice.

The soldiers stepped aside and one of them waved me on without a word, and I was passing them, no one paying me any attention. Evidently they were still looking for the black limousine and nothing else.

I was through the town ten minutes later and was working my way up the hill on the opposite side, my heart finally slowing down.

There was only one last hurdle now, before I was out of the country, and that was the border fence. But it was dark at last, and at least for a little while they would not know that I had already passed through Vyborg.

It was nearly seven o'clock when I passed a small sign which said: BORDER CHECKPOINT 2 KILOMETERS. I ground the truck to a halt, pulling it off into the ditch and dousing the headlights.

Only two kilometers, I told myself. There would be a fence and guards, but it was dark and cold. They did not know yet that I had come this far.

I jumped out of the truck, crossed the road and plunged into the woods as a gentle snow began falling.

The wind overhead in the tree tops made a noise like a thousand babies crying in the distance, and as I worked my way west, across a narrow stream and up a steep embankment on the other side, I heard some kind of animal scream to my left.

The slight wind that penetrated the deep forest was damp and bitterly cold, and as I ran I pulled out my Luger.

There was no way I was going to be stopped this close to freedom. And once across there was nothing on this earth that would stop me from returning to Washington, D.C., and avenging Hawk's death.

I had finally admitted to myself that ninety percent of my drive in this case was now being supplied by the motive of revenge. As terribly wrong as that was, I knew it would be sweet when it finally came.

Someone shouted something to my right and I stopped, dropping to my knees to listen. A moment later the shouting came again. It was at least a couple of hundred yards away and sounded like Russian, although I could not make out the words.

Crouching low I continued through the woods, careful now with every step not to make the slightest sound.

About five minutes later, I could see a light to my right and within a hundred yards I was hiding behind a wide tree looking across a fifty-yard-wide path cut through the trees along which ran a high-wire fence. The light came from the top of a guard tower two hundred yards to my right; to my left, about a kilometer or less, was another guard tower. I could see a third beyond that one, each of them equipped with a powerful spotlight.

Four soldiers were beneath the guard tower to the right trying to dig out the rear wheels of a jeep that had become stuck in the mud.

For the moment the fence line was clear of moving patrols, and unless I made my move now, I figured, I might never get the chance again.

I stuffed my Luger back into its holster, took out my tool kit and pulled out the diamond-edged wire cutters, which I held in my mouth. Then, I got down on my belly and began crawling through the short grass out from the relative safety of the woods.

Fifty yards on this side of the fence and twenty-five or thirty yards on the other side had been cleared and was fairly well lit. So even if I made it to the fence and then through it, I still would not be home free. Somehow I was going to have to make it all the way to the woods on the other side.

Twenty-five yards from the fence the jeep to my right started up and I could hear the wheels spinning as the driver tried to rock it free from where it was stuck.

I waited for a few seconds until they shut the jeep's engine off, then I continued crawling as the snow increased in intensity.

The guard tower to my right loomed high overhead, and I was sure that at any moment I would be spotted and they would open fire. But then I was at the fence and was cutting through the wires, one at a time.

The jeep started up again and this time, after just a few seconds, it became free.

I had a hole large enough to crawl through, when a siren began to wail and a powerful spotlight stabbed the darkness toward me. I pushed my way through the hole, pulled out Wilhelmina and rolled over twice as machine-gun fire started up, kicking up the mud all around me and whining off the fence wires.

The jeep was screaming at high power coming my way as I rolled over on my back, took careful aim and fired once and then twice—my second shot knocking out the spotlight on top of the guard tower.

And then I was running and falling and stumbling across the open space, toward the woods, as bullets whined around me.

Just as I was diving into a line of brush, something hot and very hard slammed into my back and then I was rolling and tumbling down a hill, my head spinning around and around.

SEVENTEEN

He had known for some time what was going on but he had no way of proving it, nor had he any way of helping Nick Carter.

From the third floor room in the Dupont Plaza Hotel he had been watching the entrance of the Amalgamated Press Building, front for AXE headquarters, for ten days now. And he would continue to watch the building until Carter showed up, or until he learned for certain that the AXE Killmaster was dead.

During his nearly two weeks at the hotel, the old man had begun writing what he called an Agency Safeguard Manual. In it, he had set down everything he had learned over the years in the hope that when this business was finally over with, nothing like it could ever happen again.

He laid the binoculars down on the table beside the Ruger snub-nosed .44 magnum pistol and went back to his writing, glancing out the window every now and then as someone entered or left the building.

I gave the Red Cap at Washington National Airport a dollar tip and then crawled stiffly into the back seat of the cab next to my single suitcase, the pain coming at me so hard now it blurred my vision.

The cabby was looking at me in his rearview mirror, and when I had the door closed he turned around. "Are you all right buddy?"

I nodded. "Amalgamated Press, on Dupont Circle," I said. My voice was hoarse and very soft. It was difficult for me to talk or even to take a deep breath because of the wound in my back.

The machine-gun bullet had cracked two of my ribs, passing just beneath my left lung, and had lodged itself between my spleen and kidney.

The doctor in Simola had insisted that I be taken immediately to the hospital in Helsinki for an operation to remove the bullet, but I had refused. The moment I set foot in any hospital I would be a dead man.

There was very little internal bleeding, for which the doctor that Ursula had called was thankful, but he had told me I would be in constant excruciating pain.

The trip to the airport in Helsinki the next day had been a nightmare. And at this moment I could only vaguely remember changing planes in Paris and the long, overnight flight across the Atlantic.

But now everything was very nearly over with. I had come this far, nothing would stop me from finishing it.

The cab merged smoothly with traffic on the George Washington Memorial Parkway, and as we passed over the Pentagon Lagoon Bridge, north toward the Arlington Memorial Bridge, I managed to unlatch my suitcase and raise the lid.

Inside was a collection of clothing, mostly old rags that Ursula had hastily packed for me so that I would not attract the attention of customs. I pulled these out and dumped them on the floor.

The cabby had been watching me in the rearview mirror. "Hey, what the hell are you doing back there?" he said.

"Just drive," I croaked. "There'll be a big tip in it for you."

"That's fine, but I don't want my cab messed up, mister," he snapped.

I grabbed a corner of the bottom lining of the suitcase and ripped it open, and from the metal stays in each corner I removed the tape holding the parts of my Luger and the one clip of nine millimeter ammunition.

"I don't know what the hell you're doing back there, but you're getting out of my cab, tip or no tip," the cabby said, and he pulled over to the side of the road.

The barrel and slide snapped into place, and the ejector spring went into its slot, along with the retainer sleeve. As the cab came to a complete halt and the driver started to turn around, I shoved the clip into the butt, levered a round into the chamber and held the gun up in the man's face.

"Amalgamated Press. Dupont Circle," I said softly, but my hand was shaking so bad from the pain that throbbed through my body with every heartbeat, that it was difficult to hold the gun up.

"I—" the cabby started to say, but he swallowed the word.

"Amalgamated Press," I said. "Or I will kill you right now."

The cabby turned back to the wheel and eased out in traffic, as I slumped back in the seat, sweat starting to form on my forehead.

Just a little longer, I told myself. Just a few more minutes. I would have to hang on. It was too important.

I took off the blond wig, removed the glasses, the thick mustache and heavy beard and threw them on the floor.

We crossed the Potomac on the Arlington Bridge, went past the Lincoln Memorial and then up Twenty-third Street to Washington Circle, where the driver took New Hampshire Avenue.

I laid the Luger on my lap and pulled out a hundred dollar bill from my wallet, the last of the American money that Hakkala had managed to come up with for me, wadded it up and tossed it over the back of the front seat.

"Keep the change," I said softly.

The driver said nothing and a couple of minutes later we pulled up in front of the Amalgamated Press building.

"Thanks for the ride," I said, and I opened the door and crawled painfully out of the cab, swaying on my feet for a moment as a wave of dizziness and nausea washed over me.

"What about your suitcase and this mess in here?" the cabby shouted, but I ignored him as I went across the sidewalk and entered the lobby.

Tom Briggs the day shift security guard was writing something in his log and he glanced up at me as I came through the doors. There were only two other people in the lobby, both of them women waiting for an elevator. I didn't recognize either of them, although I suspected they worked downstairs in archives.

"You'll have to sign in here, sir," Briggs started to

say, but then his eyes went wide. "Oh my God—"

I raised the Luger and pointed it at his head as he started to reach for the pistol at his hip. "Hands behind your head, Tom, and then stand up."

"Oh my God," Briggs said again, but he complied. When he was up I motioned him over to the elevators. The two women had shrunk back out of the way.

I nearly stumbled and fell halfway to the elevator, but then regained my balance, and a moment later the doors opened and we stepped inside.

"What are you going to do, Mr. Carter?" Briggs asked.

I nodded toward the panel. "Top floor," I said.

After a brief hesitation Briggs reached out and hit the button for the top floor, and the elevator started up.

"You're going to come with me, Tom, and I'm going to ask you to listen to everything that is said," I croaked. "Do you understand?"

Briggs nodded, his Adam's apple bobbing up and down.

Less than a minute later the elevator doors slid open and Briggs started to step out. Mandel was waiting at his office door just behind his secretary's desk, a pistol in his hand, and he fired, hitting Briggs in the chest.

In the next instant I fired two shots. The first hit Mandel in the stomach and the second in his throat, which erupted in a mass of blood, and he was flung backward into his office.

Then the floor seemed to tilt upward at a crazy angle. It seemed as if someone had knocked over the building, because I was watching the ceiling slide over to where the wall should have been. And then nothing.

EPILOGUE

"Mandel was a mole," David Hawk said. He was sitting across the glass-topped table from me by the swimming pool at AXE's recovery hospital and ranch outside Phoenix, Arizona.

I had been in intensive care at Bethesda Naval Hospital in Washington for ten days after they had removed the bullet from my back, and another thirty days before I had been moved down here.

During that time I had not been debriefed, although Hawk had visited me nearly every day and even the President had telephoned.

The agency historians, budget men and cleanup operations people would be coming down here later today, and they figured it probably would take a week or more to get the entire affair down on paper and straightened out.

"How did you figure it out?" I asked. My voice was still weak.

Hawk shrugged. "I suspected Mandel almost from the beginning, but each step of the way everything pointed to him more and more. Like finding you in Paris and planting the bomb in your hotel room. Our own people could not have caught up with you so fast. We didn't have enough legmen. But Mandel was not only directing AXE and the CIA in the search, he was dividing the work with his own KGB people. Three secret services were looking for you. The KGB happened to get to you first."

"Why didn't you tell me when I called?" I asked.

"I wasn't completely sure at that point. If I had told you that I suspected Mandel, you might not have believed me."

I started to protest, but then cut it off. He was right.

"I had a couple of old friends, who had been in the French underground network during the war, come up with a fresh body from the city morgue and plant it in your room to slow Mandel and his people down a bit. Give you a little breathing room."

The presence of that extra body had bothered me through the entire business. I had had visions of Hawk ordering the cold-blooded murder of someone to act as a cover for me. I was relieved that had not been the case.

"What happened at your cabin then?" I asked. "When I called Mandel was there."

"After you phoned me from Paris, I knew that the cabin wouldn't be safe any longer, so I hid in the woods and waited around to see who would show up first."

"KGB?" I asked, and Hawk nodded as he lit himself a cigar and puffed deeply.

"I recognized one of them from the Washington

Embassy staff. When they didn't find me, they left and a couple of hours later a team of AXE technicians showed up, dusted the place for prints and then fixed the telephone so that incoming calls would be routed to Mandel's office.''

"At that point you knew for certain Mandel was a mole?" I asked.

Hawk nodded. "It would have done no good to expose him at that point, however. We had no proof. I had to wait for you. Even now that we know for certain he was a mole, we're having trouble unraveling his background. They did a damned fine job of building him a cover.''

I took a sip of my drink, then lit myself a cigarette and closed my eyes.

"When did you know for sure it was Mandel?" Hawk was asking.

"I never suspected him until the end," I admitted. "The CIA tumbled to me in Helsinki, and when I got to Moscow I found out that the KGB had been informed I was coming in. The only way for them to know that for sure, was a leak. The CIA told Mandel and Mandel told his bosses at Dzerzhinsky Square. It was the only possibility.''

For a long time after that we sat in silence. It had been a brilliant plan that had very nearly succeeded. If Hawk and I had both been killed, Mandel would have been able to give the Soviets all of our secrets and there would have been no one to suspect him. The enormity of it was frightening.

And now what, I asked myself. There was Kazuka Akiyama and Sandry Triggs. I had made promises to both of them, and somehow I was going to have to work that out without hurting them too badly.

I was not getting out of AXE. Not now. Not ever.

FROM THE NICK CARTER

KILLMASTER SERIES

☐ TEMPLE OF FEAR	80215-X	$1.75
☐ THE NICHOVEV PLOT	57435-1	$1.75
☐ TIME CLOCK OF DEATH	81025-X	$1.75
☐ UNDER THE WALL	84499-6	$1.75
☐ THE PEMEX CHART	65858-X	$1.95
☐ SIGN OF THE PRAYER SHAWL	76355-3	$1.75
☐ THUNDERSTRUCK IN SYRIA	80860-3	$1.95
☐ THE MAN WHO SOLD DEATH	51921-0	$1.75
☐ THE SUICIDE SEAT	79077-1	$2.25
☐ SAFARI OF SPIES	75330-2	$1.95
☐ TURKISH BLOODBATH	82726-8	$2.25
☐ WAR FROM THE CLOUDS	87192-5	$2.25
☐ THE JUDAS SPY	41295-5	$1.75

NICK CARTER

> "Nick Carter out-Bonds James Bond."
> —*Buffalo Evening News*

Exciting, international espionage adventure with Nick Carter, Killmaster N3 of AXE, the super-secret agency!

TRIPLE CROSS   82407-2 $1.95
It all began as a favor—a routine hit that explodes in Nick's face!

THE SATAN TRAP   75035-4 $1.95
Nick infiltrates a religious cult whose victims are the most powerful men in Europe.

THE REDOLMO AFFAIR   71133-2 $1.95
Nick must find and kill Redolmo—the mastermind behind a drug ring that is crippling the West!

THE GREEN WOLF CONNECTION   30328-5 $1.50
Middle-eastern oil is the name of the game, and the sheiks were masters of terror.

MACAO   51354-9 $1.95
Nick's partner is the ruthless and beautiful Princess da Gama—but is catching spies her game?

THE MIND KILLERS   53298-5 $1.95
They were human time bombs, programmed to assassinate. Their next target: the U.S. president!

THE OMEGA TERROR   64053-2 $1.95
A deadly man-made organism is about to be loosed on the U.S.

Available wherever paperbacks are sold or use this coupon.

Ⓒ ACE CHARTER BOOKS
P.O. Box 400, Kirkwood, N.Y. 13795

Please send me the titles checked above. I enclose _____
Include 75¢ for postage and handling if one book is ordered; 50¢ per book for two to five. If six or more are ordered, postage is free. California, Illinois, New York and Tennessee residents please add sales tax.

NAME_____

ADDRESS_____

CITY_____STATE_____ZIP_____

N-03

CHARTER BOOKS

SUSPENSE TO KEEP YOU ON THE EDGE OF YOUR SEAT

CHARTER MYSTERIES

Stunning Thrillers You Won't Want to Miss